Dr. Morgan Talbot was too handsome by half.

Rachel could spend hours just staring at him and watching the different expressions that crossed his face, listening to his deep musical laughter.

"Time for your examination, Rachel. Surely you don't expect your daughter to be examined if you aren't?"

"Oh." Flushing, she nodded and added, "Very ingenious of you." She stood and hopped up onto the tiny pediatric table.

"Did I mention you look nice in your navy suit?"

Her color inched up a notch. "Thank you, *Doctor*."

"Now, lift your arm," he said in his professional tone.

She lifted her arm.

"Now drop it."

She dropped it. "Why?"

"I just wanted to see if you'd do it."

Rachel smacked his arm. He chuckled and so did she.

Books by Cheryl Wolverton

Love Inspired

A Matter of Trust #11
A Father's Love #20
This Side of Paradise #38
The Best Christmas Ever #47
A Mother's Love #63
*For Love of Zach #76
*For Love of Hawk #87
†What the Doctor Ordered #93

*Hill Creek, Texas
†Fairweather

CHERYL WOLVERTON

grew up in a military town, though her father was no longer in the service when she was born. She attended Tomlinson Junior High School and Lawton High School and was attending Cameron when she met her husband, Steve. After a whirlwind courtship of two weeks they became engaged. Four months later they were married, and that was over seventeen years ago.

Cheryl and Steve have two wonderful children, Christina, sixteen, and Jeremiah, thirteen. Cheryl loves having two wonderful teenagers in the house.

As for books, Cheryl has written eight novels for the Steeple Hill Love Inspired line and is currently working on new novels. Watch for her third book in the series HILL CREEK, TEXAS, as well as other surprises planned in the future. You can contact Cheryl at P.O. Box 207, Slaughter, LA 70777. She loves to hear from readers.

What the Doctor Ordered
Cheryl Wolverton

Love Inspired®

Published by Steeple Hill Books™

Special thanks and acknowledgment are given to Cheryl Wolverton for her contribution to the Fairweather miniseries.

 STEEPLE HILL BOOKS

Steeple Hill™

ISBN 0-373-87099-X

WHAT THE DOCTOR ORDERED

Copyright © 2000 by Steeple Hill Books, Fribourg, Switzerland

Visit us at www.steeplehill.com

Printed in U.S.A.

And we know that all things work together
for good to them that love God and are called
according to his purpose.

—Romans 8:28

Dedicated to all the mothers and fathers
who have been there for their kids.

Acknowledgments

James, big bro, this one is to you.
What can I say? I love you.

Sometimes there are special people who touch
your life, people you never forget. Years later
you still remember the kind deeds they did or the
gentle spirit they had. I know two such people.
Dr. Jerry Youker. Your gentle spirit, your care for
the person as a person and not just as a patient, has
never left me! The way you allowed me to follow
you around as a volunteer at Comanche County
Memorial Hospital in Lawton, Oklahoma, will
never be forgotten.

And Dr. Mogab! Oh, how I loved to be tested by
you, as you'd let me look at X rays with you and go
in rooms with you as you stitched up people! I still
have those fond memories of being student to your
teacher. Thank you both.

Chapter One

She ran right into him—literally.

Rachel Anderson White stumbled and dropped the bags she'd been carrying in her arms.

"Whoa, there." A large, strong hand reached out and steadied her. The firm, warm grip was definitely male, Rachel thought as she looked at the long, slim fingers and the dark skin that led to a well-muscled arm.

Rachel lifted her gaze to the deep brown eyes of one of the most gorgeous men she'd ever seen. She worked hard not to suck in a breath of disbelief. Dark, conservatively cut hair topped high cheekbones, straight nose and a firm, square jaw. Her gaze touched each of these features one by one before traveling to twinkling eyes that shone with warmth. When his mouth curved into a warm, friendly smile her heart thumped a bit faster.

"Are you all right?"

Rachel heard the question but stood stunned, quite unable to answer.

"Here, let me help you, Mrs....?"

The *Mrs.* snapped her out of her stupor, though she wasn't sure if it was because that word still brought pain or if she wanted him to know she wasn't married. "Miss. Rachel Anderson White. I didn't mean to nearly knock you down. I was bringing supplies for my daughter's class and not watching where I was..."

She noticed the child he carried on his left hip. Her cheeks heated as the dark-haired sparkling-eyed boy, no more than three or four years old, hugged the man and whispered something.

The hunk whispered gentle words to the child before a low chuckle filled the air around him. Glancing at Rachel, the man smiled. "He'd like me to tell you he's Jeremy and he went to ask Pastor Ben to pray for him because he's sick.''

The little boy nodded, his shaggy brown bangs falling in his eyes, reminding her of a shaggy little dog as his head bobbed excitedly.

''I...see.'' Rachel wasn't sure what to say, since she didn't attend church here and didn't really know the pastor. ''Are you feeling better?'' she asked lamely.

The child grinned and nodded. ''All better.''

Rachel chuckled. ''Well, that's good.''

Setting the young boy on his feet, the man paused to squeeze the boy's shoulders. ''Go back to class, Jeremy. You'll be fine now.''

The little boy bounced down the hall without a backward glance, his fast gait echoing loudly on the tiled floor.

''By the way, I'm Morgan—''

''I hope it's not serious?'' Rachel said at the same time.

They both laughed.

Mild panic seized her that her daughter might be exposed to something that afflicted Jeremy and she'd have to take off work when she had just gotten her new job.

Morgan shook his head. ''Not at all. He

thought he had pinkeye, but he only has a mild cold. Still he wanted Pastor Ben to pray for him before he went back for his nap.''

Nap! The relief she'd started to feel at his words was instantly replaced with more panic.

''Oh, dear.'' Rachel dropped to her knees and started gathering paper towels, a bag of finger paints, a tiny pink pillow, an apron and a ratty blue much-used blanket.

As she reached for the blanket, Morgan snatched it up, along with the paints and a box of tissues. ''Here we go,'' he said, and slipped the things into one of the bags she had been carrying. ''Are you new here?''

Rachel paused in repacking the sacks. She was used to that question. In the past week she'd heard it from at least a dozen people here in Fairweather, Minnesota. Though she'd grown up in Fairweather and knew many of the people, she found, in the years since she'd moved away, married and had a child, new people had moved in, and the town had grown and changed, despite the fact it was a small community. This man and his child were two people she didn't recognize, either. Mr. Morgan, she thought. "Yes and no," she replied, smiling noncommittally.

Standing, she reached for the bags.

He picked them up before she could. "Allow me."

Rachel bristled, but realized it was simply country manners. She'd lived in the big city too long, was used to everyone wanting something or expecting something in return, even her former husband.

Pain filled her heart at the memory. Betrayal, hurt and finally grief as she remembered the call to inform her that her husband had been killed in an auto accident. Nevertheless, that was then, this was now, a new start, a new way of things, new values. Forcing herself to relax, she nodded her thanks. "My daughter is new to the church day care," Rachel said as a peace offering. She didn't even know the new pastor. Though she'd been back almost two weeks, she'd not attended church. Her mother had informed her there was a new young pastor, but she had no desire to meet him, to hear any messages he preached, to hear anything about God. She'd bitterly learned that she had to depend on herself. Not others.

Morgan stepped back and motioned her to lead the way. "Ah, your daughter must be...Lindsay or maybe Chrissy?"

"You know the children that well?" Rachel asked, surprised.

The corners of his mouth crooked into a mischievous smile and he said, "I love kids."

She found his grin infectious. Then she remembered why she was here. And why, despite how nice looking this man was, she didn't have time for him or anyone else. She had to find herself and attempt to make a life here for Lindsay. With that in mind, Rachel strode past him and down the hall toward her daughter's class.

The sound of music, laughter, cries, blocks being banged together and teachers teaching all mingled together in a type of controlled chaos as they walked to the nursery. Rachel knew that in this noise and movement children were actually learning. Her mother said this day care had warm, caring people and was the best in the area. That's what Rachel wanted for her child. The best. The safest. In addition, it was the place least likely for Lindsay to have problems.

When they arrived at the room for three-year-olds, she searched the faces of the children for her daughter—and quickly found her.

Lindsay sat alone, in a corner, a stack of blocks in front of her as she built them up, higher and higher. The other children were in free time, but Lindsay—she acted as if she were unaware of the activity going on around her.

There was a simple explanation for that.

Lindsay was hearing impaired. Different, an oddity and shunned by many.

Including her father.

But not Rachel. Rachel loved her daughter more than life itself. That's why she'd moved back to Fairweather. A small community would be a better environment for her. She wouldn't have to put up with the many well-meaning people who continually said that Lindsay should be put in a special school. Or the ones who insisted she should have surgery—a surgery that *might* help if she would only find a doctor who could perform this amazing miracle operation that they just knew was out there for her daughter.

She'd been to Lindsay's doctor. She'd been

to her own doctor. They both agreed sending Lindsay to a special school for specific training was the first step. Later, maybe, they said, something would develop. Possibly surgery, but that probably wouldn't help. All in all, the advice was to send her off to a home somewhere so people who were trained with kids like her could deal with her. She wasn't sending her daughter away and that was that.

Julianne Quinn, who normally taught the four-year-olds, was teaching both classes today. Rachel had heard from her mother that Julianne had recently been jilted by her fiancé. Her mother wondered if perhaps that was why Julianne had been working so many hours lately. Tall, slim, with blond hair, she smiled at Rachel and moved over to touch Lindsay on the shoulder.

"Lindsay is mine," Rachel finally said, answering the man's earlier question.

"I see that," he murmured.

Rachel couldn't imagine how. Lindsay had blond hair and a round, cherubic face, just like her father had. The only thing Lindsay had inherited from Rachel was the blue eyes. Her ex-husband's eyes had been green.

Maybe it was the way Lindsay's eyes glowed as she ran to the door.

"Maanu Maanu," the little girl said, and held her arms up.

Rachel bent over the small gate and lifted her daughter into her embrace. Kissing her on the forehead, she touched the child's cheek to draw her attention to her mouth. "Mama. Mama has something for you."

Turning, Rachel reached into the sack and pulled out the blanket, ratty blue but very much loved by her daughter.

"Bae ee."

Rachel nodded, kissed her on the cheek and set her down. She added sign language to her words. "Go play, honey."

Lindsay shook her head and tapped her fingers together.

"Mama will be back later. After nap time," she said with a smile, doing what now came naturally and adding the signs for *back later* and *after sleep*.

Lindsay looked at her blocks in indecision until she saw Jeremy headed that way. Without a word, she turned and ran over to guard her territory, putting her arms around the blocks and babbling something at Jeremy.

Rachel chewed her lip, watching to see if Jeremy teased her. He didn't. He handed her some more blocks and then plopped down near her with a car and started playing.

"Jeremy made it back." Julianne said this to the man next to Rachel.

"Thanks. This is Miss White's." After handing the bags over the gate, Morgan stepped to one side.

Rachel relaxed slightly. She wasn't used to having a man distracting her and didn't like the feeling at all. "How's she doing?"

Julianne smiled. "She's doing fine. She's adjusting. I think the hearing problem is continuing to keep her isolated from others. But a few of the more curious children have started trying to talk to her."

"Children can be mean."

Julianne nodded and said softly, "Or they can be the breakthrough. Earlier today, she sat near Chrissy and they shared an apple."

Rachel nodded.

"Your daughter's deaf?" Morgan asked, drawing Rachel's attention to him.

"Partially. A degenerative thing." Rachel didn't like to talk to strangers about her daughter. And this was a stranger. "Excuse me. I have to get back to work."

She smiled politely at the man and then said to Julianne, "If you need me, just call City Hall. I'll be there another hour or two before I'm back to pick Lindsay up. Nice meeting you," she said to the man and then waved to Julianne and started down the hall.

Morgan watched her leave, unmoving.

"She's really good with her daughter, just a little overprotective, Dr. Talbot."

Hearing Julianne's voice, he realized he was still staring after the exceptional woman. He tried to force his attention from Rachel White but couldn't bring himself to let her out of his sight. When she turned the corner, he finally turned his attention to Julianne. "Most parents are. Parents with handicapped children have emotions that most can't understand."

A touch of melancholy swept over him. Shaking his head, he forced the feeling aside. "If you need me again, just call. I have to get back to work."

A smile touched the woman's lips, and she

nodded. The sound of a squabble caught their attention, and Julianne was off to handle the problem.

Morgan walked down the hall, intending to leave. Instead, he stopped at the end of the hall by the window that overlooked the square. Pushing the curtain back, he located exactly what had captured his attention and watched her continue across the green toward City Hall.

"Caught you!"

Ben Hunter came walking up.

Morgan turned, allowing the shade to drop. "Caught me what?"

Ben pulled the curtain back and glanced out. "Daydreaming? Thinking about Jeremy or perhaps one of the other children that'll be lined up in your office in the next thirty minutes or so?"

Morgan shook his head and smiled. "No, not that. Not at all."

"Oh?" Ben asked and turned toward his office, motioning Morgan to accompany him.

Morgan followed Pastor Ben, who continued, "So, what was it you were doing?"

Ben paused outside his office and turned the

door handle, his gaze touching on Morgan's in query.

Morgan decided, Why not tell Pastor Ben the truth? Taking a deep breath, he said, his voice low, "I was studying the woman I am going to marry."

Chapter Two

"I didn't realize you were even dating any-one," Reverend Ben said.

"Dating? Who's dating someone?" Emma Fulton, Ben's secretary, asked.

Ben nodded to Emma as he passed through the secretary's office and walked into his own office. Morgan watched, amused. Emma Fulton was sixty-five years old, but he certainly couldn't tell it by her actions. Patting her strawberry-blond hair, which was more white than red, she tucked an imaginary loose strand into the braid that was twirled in a bun on top of her head. She got up and followed the pastor toward his office, her matchmaking antennae zeroing in. "You know, Julianne's fiancé left her. That was such a shame. Now there's a woman who needs someone."

Morgan saw the look on Emma's face, the gleam in her eye and thought, Yep, the pastor was certainly in trouble.

"In God's time, Emma," Ben said gently. "So, what messages do you have for me?"

"Oh. Yes. Yes." Looking at the slips in her hand, she said, "Well, Miss Patterson called and I think she wanted, or was it the other one that wanted..." The woman trailed off, confused, quickly looking through the notes she held in her aged hands.

"Take your time, Emma," Ben soothed and seated himself, motioning for Morgan to take a chair also.

"No, no. It was Rachel's mother who called in reference to the roofing project you wanted to know about. And Miss Patterson, she wanted to talk to you about sponsoring." The woman frowned as she tried to remember. "Oh, yes. She wanted to talk with you about sponsoring a booth at the celebration they'll be having, the spring festival. You know, I was crowned Strawberry Queen at that festival years ago.'' She gleamed with pride as she nodded to Morgan.

''I'd heard that, ma'am,'' Morgan replied, smiling. Actually, he'd heard it several times from Emma. It was something she was very proud of, and every time the spring festival came up, she mentioned it. ''Quite an event,'' he added.

She giggled.

Taking the messages from Emma, Ben paused to pat her hand. ''Thank you, dear. Can you close the door on the way out?''

''I surely will, Reverend Ben.'' She turned and bustled out the door, her mission thwarted temporarily but, knowing Emma, not deserted.

When the door finally clicked closed, Morgan chuckled. ''Looks like you may be fighting off a matchmaking scheme there, Ben.''

Ben groaned and shook his head. ''Emma's a good woman. She certainly cares about everyone. But I draw the line at allowing her to pick my wife.'' Smiling, he shook his head again.

Morgan chuckled again.

Ben's blue eyes gleamed with amusement as he said, ''You don't have much room to laugh, Morgan. She's tried to match you up with every single woman within a three-county area.''

''Yeah, but she's turned that attention on you now. Looks like she's given me up as a lost cause—at least temporarily.'' Morgan's smile faded. ''So, how are the problems going?''

Ben shook his head and laid the messages aside. ''Still getting a lot of opposition from many in the church. I'm too young to handle this job, according to some. Others think the former Reverend shouldn't have retired and let someone with my lack of experience slip into the job. In time, though, I'm sure, with God's help, things will change.''

''Good.'' Morgan shifted in his chair and crossed his legs. In khaki pants and a deep blue polo shirt, he felt as if he were missing something. Normally, he wore a lab coat and stethoscope, too. He'd been at lunch when he'd gotten paged to come over because the day care was certain Jeremy had pinkeye. ''By the way, that's not pinkeye,'' he said to Ben. ''It seems Chrissy didn't like what Jeremy said and punched him in the eye while the teacher's back was turned. But Jeremy heard the teacher say pinkeye and was certain his eye was going to turn pink and fall out.''

"Oh, really?'' Ben grinned, the lines around his eyes crinkling in amusement. ''Well, I'm sure he'll think a miracle occurred when his eye clears.''

''And his mom will be glad to know the sniffles aren't going to turn into anything more. So, what'd you want to talk to me about?''

Ben grinned. ''I'd wanted to talk business, but first, I want to find out who you've been dating while my back was turned.''

Morgan glanced at Ben's desk, cluttered with books and notes, the books obviously from the many bookcases around the office. The church was an old building, with original wood paneling and floors. Beautiful, in a way. Morgan really liked it, and liked his pastor, too. He'd become a friend over the last few months through the church-run day care. He wondered how he was going to explain to Ben what he'd meant earlier. Oh, well, he thought. I made the statement, might as well explain it. ''Her name is Rachel and she has a daughter...''

''Lindsay,'' Ben finished. ''Yes. I've seen

her picking Lindsay up, and of course, know her mother, Betty. I didn't know *you* knew her, though. Or is it that Betty introduced you two?''

Morgan grinned. ''No, Betty has no idea I've met her daughter yet. And I don't know Rachel yet, either.''

''I see,'' Ben replied, though it was perfectly obvious he didn't see at all.

''I met her a few minutes ago,'' Morgan added, not offering more than a simple blink of his eyes in reaction to the total confusion written on Ben's face.

''Ah.'' Ben chuckled, his face clearing suddenly. Morgan knew Ben thought he was kidding. Let him think that—until he finally asked Ben to perform the ceremony. He couldn't explain it himself, but when he'd seen Rachel his entire world had tilted on its axis. A strong voice inside had spoken to him, saying, She's the one. Morgan had no problem agreeing. She was beautiful, but there was something more about her, something he couldn't explain. He simply knew she was the woman who belonged at his side, and he was going to marry her.

He was rather stunned himself, in some

ways. He wasn't one to make rash decisions. Actually, he was usually very controlled and careful. Nevertheless, he knew, he *knew* she was the one.

And Lindsay.

The child only confirmed what he knew. She was for him. Lindsay was for him. A second chance…

"Well, since you brought Rachel up…" Ben broke into the silence, his laughter gone as he drew Morgan to the subject at hand. "Betty called while you were checking on Jeremy. She was looking for you."

"Really?" Betty Anderson, the director of the day-care center, was also Rachel's mom. "What does she want to see me about?"

"I don't know. I told her I'd snag you before you left. Let me tell her you're here." He picked up the phone and rang the day-care office. When he hung up, he smiled at Morgan. "She's on her way now."

"No measles going around, at least, not that I know of. Maybe she wants me to set up the annual lice check, or…" Morgan trailed off, curious.

"I'm sure it's something like that. You know Betty. She's an exceptional woman, good head on her shoulders. She certainly keeps that day care in line.''

Morgan nodded. "That she does. And knowing her, she'll waste no time getting here and coming to the point.'' Morgan liked that about Betty.

As if on cue, they heard Emma in the other room, offering a strawberry-filled cookie to someone and talking about seeing her daughter. "Sounds like Betty is here," Morgan said.

Ben stood and moved around his desk. "I'll give you some privacy." He laid a gentle hand on Morgan's shoulder as he passed. Morgan heard the door click and the warm tones of Ben's voice float to him from the secretary's office. "Hello, Betty. Morgan is in my office. Go on in. In the meantime, I think I'm going to steal one of Emma's cookies.''

"Thank you, Reverend.'' Betty's contralto voice could be heard. A breeze swept in as the door swung wider, and then Betty walked in the office.

Betty pushed the door closed and stood there, her reddish brown hair hanging straight to her chin. In her fifties, she still had a nice figure. Her no-nonsense clothes showed she'd evidently been doing something physical downstairs at the center. Her flannel shirt-sleeves were rolled to her elbows, and her purple jogging pants had dust and debris on them.

The look in her eye indicated that something was definitely on her mind. As a doctor, Morgan had learned to recognize the signs and do much what a pastor did, which was simply to listen. "Hello, Betty, how can I help you?"

He stood and put his hands to the back of a chair, offering Betty a seat.

"Thanks, Morgan." Betty strode across the room and seated herself. "Sit down. I need to talk to you." Betty sat on the edge of her seat and leaned forward, facing Morgan as he re-seated himself. Concern furrowed her brow, and her hands clasped around her knees. Morgan had never seen this side of Betty before.

"Now, you know I'm not one to usually interfere in my children's lives. Neither Ray nor I were, bless his soul. When I lost him five years ago... Well, let's just say I'm not sure where I would be now without my kids' support. But my daughter Rachel..."

Morgan was more than a little interested when Betty hesitated. "I met her today," he offered, hoping to put her at ease.

"Oh?" She studied him. Her gaze was so

direct that he had the distinct feeling she was looking right into his soul.

"Yes, ma'am."

"Have you met Lindsay?"

"Yes. Well, actually, I've only seen her. I haven't had time to talk with her, if that's what you mean."

"She's almost completely deaf," Betty said bluntly. "And I think my daughter is so steeped in bitterness over her husband leaving her and then dying on her that she can't see past that. He left her because of Lindsay, saying he couldn't handle a damaged child, you know."

"Ah," Morgan said, not having known that at all. So that was why Rachel had acted so prickly. She didn't trust men. Morgan couldn't blame her if what Betty had just told him was true. Most of the mothers he knew were very protective of their children and very vulnerable, too. "I'm sure Rachel will work through it and fall in love again."

Betty blinked. "Oh, Rachel? Oh, no, Morgan, I wanted to talk to you about my granddaughter. I was just filling you in on Rachel so you'd know where I was coming from. You see, she's very protective of Lindsay. I think

Rachel's husband killed something in her when he rejected their daughter. Rachel went to a doctor, but the brainless fool suggested she put her child in an institution since her husband had left her. He was not a good man. Why she went to a doctor her husband suggested, I'll never know. The doctor told Rachel it was a degenerative disease and that Lindsay should be put in an institution where she'd get more stable care than a working mother could give her. Told her that way she'd have someone who knew how to deal with deaf children.''

Shocked, Morgan stared at Betty. He could see the anger as Betty's mouth tightened in disgust. He found it hard not to feel a bit disgusted himself. Of course, sometimes family didn't know the whole story. ''Do you know what type of tests they did on Lindsay? What brought the doctor to this conclusion?''

''Other than the fact that the doctor was a real close friend of Lindsay's former husband and ran in the same circles he did?'' Betty shook her head. ''I'm sorry, Morgan. This subject really gets to me.''

Morgan could see that. ''What would you

like me to do? I could make an appointment for Lindsay and talk to Rachel—"

"Oh, no. That won't work." Betty sat back in her chair, resting her elbows on the arms. "Rachel has sworn off doctors for her child. She refuses to allow any of them to examine Lindsay anymore. I think, Morgan, she's afraid that they'll try to take her child away from her, or call her a bad mother again, or even give her hope where there is none. She worked hard to find someone to see Lindsay, to prove to her husband her child wasn't damaged. None of it did a bit of good. He left her anyway."

Morgan nodded, definitely feeling anger stir in him, anger and painful loss. "I haven't seen Rachel in church," Morgan said softly to Betty.

Hurt flashed in Betty's eyes. "She wants nothing to do with God. She's hurting, possibly even blaming God that she had a child that broke up her marriage. I've heard her say a couple of times she doesn't think God takes a real interest in her life."

Frowning, Morgan nodded. He'd been through that at one time. He was still going through it in some ways. But he had not turned his back on God. He struggled a lot with believing God had forgiven him for past sins. When someone was hurting, it was the same principle. They looked back at the pain and had trouble letting go. So he could understand where Rachel might still be hurting and hadn't let go.

"Well, then, if it's not an appointment you want, what is it you need?"

Betty smiled. "I have a plan...."

Seeing that smile, Morgan wondered if he had just stepped off a cliff and was heading toward imminent disaster on the rocky beach below.

Chapter Three

"**W**hy wasn't he at supper last week if this is such a regular event?"

Rachel rushed around, picking up clothes, shoes and toys that Lindsay had dragged out. She was unable to believe what her mother was telling her.

"Because, Rachel," Betty said, pulling a chicken out of the oven and setting it on the stove, "you were moving in and things were hectic. I often have members of the church over here to eat two or three times a week. However, I didn't want to invite anyone until you had gotten your things moved in. In addition, he's single. I feel responsible for him.

He needs a good home-cooked meal every once in a while.''

"He?" Rachel asked, tossing the miscellaneous articles into her bedroom and pulling the door shut. "And why do you feel responsible? Does he have a kid in your day care?"

Rachel knew her mom loved to mother everyone. All the kids at the day care she thought of as hers. If there was a single father who was having a rough time of it, she wouldn't be the least bit surprised to find out her mother had adopted him and was having him over for dinner all the time. Rachel's mind drifted to the appealing man she'd met earlier that day.

"No. He's a big help there, though."

Scratch that one. Rachel wasn't sure if she was relieved or disappointed. Dropping to her knees, she started gathering blocks from the round wool carpet that covered the floor. That was all they needed—someone to come in and break their neck on a block.

"Maa uh!" Lindsay came running into the room and launched herself onto Rachel's back.

"Umph." Rachel, precariously balanced, went down, blocks going everywhere.

Lindsay gurgled and crawled onto her mom, bouncing. "Pae-ee. Pae-ee."

She waved her hands, motioning.

"Not now," Rachel signed. "Cleaning."

"Pae-ee."

Rachel started to shake her head and say no again, but saw the look of laughter in her daughter's eyes. How often had she had time to play with her daughter in the last month? She'd had to put their house up for sale in the twin cities, get things packed up, move, find a job here. She'd tried to be there for her daughter, but tonight, she'd been longer than she'd planned and then had had to run errands for her mother. She had taken a long shower only to come down to find out they were having company.

Company.

She just didn't have the time....

"Go on, take a quick break. You have time, honey," her mother called from the kitchen.

They did have twenty more minutes, she thought.

Lindsay bounced on her.

Rachel oofed for her daughter.

Lindsay squealed, delighted.

Rachel gave in. Just a minute wouldn't matter. "Mommies tickle for that." She signed as she said it.

Lindsay squealed again and promptly bounced once more.

"Mommies gobble, too." Rachel followed this with actions as she grabbed her daughter and pulled her up, searching for her tummy under her shirt before blowing raspberries.

Lindsay shrieked and laughed. "Mo! Mo!"

"You want more, do you, you little munchkin?" she said, bouncing Lindsay on her tummy. "Okay, here it comes." She lifted her hand and started twisting it around, making a buzzing noise.

Lindsay's hand went to her mother's mouth to feel the sensations.

Rachel twisted her finger again. "Zzzzzz…here it comes. Zzzzz…"

Giggling, Lindsay wiggled, but Rachel wouldn't release her. "I got you now, bubble baby," she teased and then dived in, grabbing Lindsay's tummy and tickling. Lindsay glowed as she laughed and slapped at her mommy's hands. In fact, she was so loud Rachel didn't hear the doorbell. All she saw was her mother pass by.

It was Lindsay who alerted her to the newcomer. Her eyes lost the gleam and focused toward the door. "Maaamuuu." She pointed at her grandmother.

Tilting her head to look at her mother and see what she wanted, Rachel realized it wasn't MaMu her daughter was pointing at. Lindsay was telling her that someone else was here.

And of course, it would be the one person she hadn't been expecting, the very person who set her heart rushing at dangerous speeds. Tall, dark and handsome stood with Betty by the door, smiling indulgently at her and Lindsay.

Chapter Four

"Good evening."

Morgan stared at her, with Lindsay sitting on her, and couldn't hide his smile. Rachel was beautiful. Flushed, her hair a mess, love glowing in her eyes for her daughter. Morgan didn't think he'd ever seen a more perfect picture of motherhood.

"Uh..."

And she was embarrassed, he realized.

Sitting up, she lifted Lindsay with her. "Wash. Dinner," she said to her daughter, and Morgan was surprised to see how easily she used American Sign Language right along with her words. In all his years of practice, he'd had a few deaf children. Few mothers bothered to learn how to communicate with their deaf children, other than to point.

Lindsay cast another glance at Morgan and sprinted toward the bathroom.

Rachel stood and smoothed her charcoal trousers. The thin blue sweater she wore had just a hint of gray to bring out the blue in her eyes. He didn't feel overdressed in his gray pants and sweater. He'd debated long and hard what to wear and had finally given up and pulled this outfit out of the closet. Morgan couldn't remember a time he'd been worried about how he looked for a woman.

Rachel was different.

"Hello again."

She glanced around him curiously, and he wondered what she was looking for. "Where's your child?"

The question hit him in the gut. How could she know...

"Jeremy?"

"Oh." Morgan relaxed. Offering a generous smile, he said, "Jeremy wasn't mine."

She quirked her brow in query, but Lindsay chose that moment to come running into the room. "Unre, maauu."

"Time for dinner," she said and lifted her daughter into her arms.

"I had no idea Betty was your mother when I met you today." He quirked his lips apologetically.

Rachel returned the smile with a halfhearted nod. "Well, she is. And we're living with her for a while."

She tilted her head toward her daughter, and her hair fell, covering her face. Long delicate fingers came up and absently pushed it behind her ear. "Aren't we, Lindsay?" she sing-songed softly as she started to the table. "Please, come in and have a seat. Make yourself at home. Mom tells me you're over here quite a bit."

Morgan followed her into the dining room and watched as she strapped her daughter into a child's seat before grabbing a sipper cup and setting it in front of her daughter. "Yes, your mom has adopted me."

Betty, who was coming in with the chicken, nodded. "I sure did. He's my local son, since both of you kids never come visit your mama."

Morgan went over and took the platter from her. "Let me get that, Betty."

"Thanks, Morgan." She turned to go into the kitchen, talking over her shoulder. "Sit down, get aquainted. I'll be right back."

Morgan hesitated then nodded. Looking at Rachel, he said, "Very self-reliant, isn't she?"

Rachel chuckled. "Understatement." She got up, got the napkins and silverware and finished setting the table.

"You know sign language well."

Rachel glanced at him in surprise. "My daughter is hearing impaired," she replied simply.

"How much does she understand?" he queried.

Rachel frowned. "Enough."

He heard it in her voice. Back off. So he did, turning his attention to Lindsay instead.

She was sipping, staring at him over the rim as she drank her juice.

Morgan grinned at her and signed, "Hi. I'm Morgan. You like juice?"

The little girl stared at him suspiciously over the cup before she tossed it at him and signed, "Share!"

Morgan caught it in midair. It was pure luck. He hadn't expected her to throw her cup at him.

"Lindsay!" Rachel said and hurried toward her daughter.

Morgan looked at Lindsay.

She giggled.

He tried to cover a smile. "Thank you," he signed, and acted as if he were taking a drink before handing it back to her.

"I'm sorry, Mr. Morgan—"

"Just Morgan."

"Okay, just Morgan," Rachel said, exasperated. "Will you stop grinning at her? She's going to think it's okay to throw her cup at you all the time."

"She was only sharing," he said innocently.

Rachel, who'd had her back turned during the entire incident, paused and looked from one to the other. "She normally doesn't talk to strangers."

"She knows me," he said, signing with his words.

Rachel's jaw dropped. "You know sign language?"

"Yes, Rachel, I do. We were talking while you were digging for the coasters. I asked her if she liked her juice, and she shared it with me. I take that to mean either she likes me and decided to be my friend or she hates her juice.''

Rachel studied him again before her gaze went to her daughter, who was sipping her juice. Then she laughed. "I guess she decided you're a friend."

Betty chose that moment to come in with bread and vegetables. "Rachel, honey, will you get the salad and pitcher for me?"

"I can do that, Betty," Morgan said, but Rachel shook her head.

"I'll get it. I have to get her bib anyway."

She left and Morgan took the dishes from Betty and set them on the table.

"There we go, my baby. I made corn for you tonight. And carrots. Your favorite," Betty said to her granddaughter.

Lindsay smiled beatifically at her grandmother and then yelled loudly. He had to give Betty credit. For not being around the child much, she did well not to flinch when Lindsay shouted her pleasure.

Rachel returned and set the salad and pitcher on the table before slipping the bib on. When she sat down, Betty turned to Morgan. "Will you say the prayer, dear?"

Morgan didn't miss the uncomfortable shift

Rachel made. He bowed his head. "Heavenly Father, thank You for the food You've blessed us with and thank You for the company and the special precious gift You gave us in Lindsay. Bless this food, in Jesus's name, amen."

When he opened his eyes, Rachel was staring at him blankly. He returned the stare with one of warmth. Her gaze wobbled with tenderness and surprise before she glanced away. "Lindsay is certainly my precious gift," she said, then proceeded to dish up a plate of food for her child.

After handing Lindsay her silverware, Rachel cut her daughter's chicken and broke up the bread, then started filling her own plate.

Morgan filled his quietly. "I found a new fishing hole, Betty."

"Oh? Where this time?"

Morgan passed Betty the platter of meat as he said, "Outside of town. The mile road. You go down it and it's off west about a mile."

"The old Henderson place. They had a creek running back there."

"I'm planning to go soon. Joe Pierceson told me about it."

"He'd know. That man loves to fish."

"Have you ever fished, Rachel?" Morgan asked politely before taking a bite of chicken.

Startled, she glanced from her daughter, her mouth filled with food. She swallowed, took a sip of tea then replied, "I haven't been in four, maybe five years." Her gaze unfocused briefly. "I used to go with Dad all the time before I went off...."

She glowed with good memories. Morgan was enchanted as he watched her.

"I remember some of the things you brought home, young lady, and it wasn't just fish. Turtles, frogs, tadpoles and even a snake. Land sakes, I'm glad that thing wasn't poisonous," Betty said.

Rachel grinned at her mother. "Daddy was, too."

Both burst out laughing, and Betty turned to Morgan to explain. "She was upset because she hadn't caught anything and her brother had. So she was walking back to the car and found this snake. A king snake, mind you, and she stuffed it into her plastic wading pants, planning to sneak it into the room and put it in her brother's bed."

"And? Did you do it?" He grinned at Rachel, whose cheeks turned pink in response.

"Go on, tell him what happened, Rachel."

"Mother." Rachel drawled the word in exasperation. "The snake got out of the trousers. Just as Daddy was pulling into the driveway, he felt something inching up the leg of his pants and panicked."

"Oh, no." Morgan couldn't help the chuckle that escaped. "Did the poor man have a heart attack?"

"Almost," Betty said. "He went right through the garage door trying to shake the thing off of his leg."

"And I got grounded for a week."

"That's pretty mild," Morgan replied, still laughing.

"Yeah. Well, I think Dad and Mom were so happy that the snake wasn't poisonous that I got off lightly."

Betty shook her head and took another bite.

Rachel grinned at her mother. "Well, Mom? You gonna tell me the truth why?"

"I have no idea why you got off so easily, dear. You're probably right. It was simply shock and relief."

Rachel chuckled again before turning to her meal. That set the tone for supper. Silly stories about her childhood. Dinner ended much too soon, as far as Morgan was concerned, but Betty wasn't about to let him leave yet. "You two go into the living room with Lindsay. I'll clear this and then bring in hot tea."

Rachel, who was cleaning Lindsay, glanced at him, then at her mom. "Okay."

Morgan nevertheless gathered his and Rachel's plates and carried them into the kitchen. When he returned, Lindsay was clean and getting out of her chair.

"So, Rachel, where do you work?" he asked, heading into the living room.

"Temporarily at City Hall. I'm reworking their records. And—watch out!"

Thump. Two little arms were wrapped around his legs. Morgan struggled to keep from landing face first on the floor. "Aha! I've been attacked," he said, peeling her arms away and lifting her. "Was it you?"

Lindsay patted his cheek and bounced in his arm. "Paaee," she said, her hand on his cheek.

"Paaee?"

"That means play. Here, I'll take her. I'm really sorry—"

"We're fine," he said to Rachel and moved to the sofa to sit down. He didn't miss how Rachel nervously followed him.

"What do you like to play, little one?" he asked.

Lindsay grinned and moved her hand to his lips.

He repeated the question.

She giggled and then stroked his cheek again.

Poor Rachel was turning all shades of red. He ignored her and continued to concentrate on Lindsay, thinking it best if he didn't pay attention to her embarrassment over her daughter. The only way Rachel would see Lindsay wasn't irritating him was to watch them together.

He reached up and put Lindsay's hand close to his mouth. "Morgan. Morgan," he said. Lifting his hand from hers, he signed, "My name. Morgan."

"Oh gan."

Morgan grinned. "Yes. Now what do you like to play? Oh, I bet I know...."

And Morgan proceeded to drop onto the floor next to the blocks and build an entire city with her for the next fifteen minutes.

Betty came in and grinned. "You're so good with kids. Lindsay has taken a liking to you. Now, Rachel, why don't you pour the tea."

"Okay, Mom." Rachel poured three cups, silently frustrated with her mother that she insisted on keeping this man around. She didn't know him, and he was playing with her daughter.

"I think little one here is getting tired," Morgan whispered.

Rachel glanced over and flushed anew. Lindsay had crawled onto him and was sprawled out, her eyes closed. "I'm sorry," Rachel began.

"Don't be." Morgan's eyes met hers. The deep tones of his voice went right through her. "I can't tell you when I've had this much fun. It's been a long time."

Rachel shifted, trying not to notice how good he looked holding her daughter. She stood and went over to him. "I should get her to bed."

Gently, she slipped her hands under her daughter and lifted the girl to her shoulder. Lindsay mumbled something and zonked right back out.

Morgan stood. "As much as I'd like tea, Betty, I really have to be up early. I should be going, too."

"Of course, Morgan. Let me take her, Rachel, and you walk our guest to the door."

Sharply, Rachel looked at her mother. *Matchmaking?*

She had to wonder. This man was attractive. Her mother didn't like it that she was alone with a child to raise. Rachel would have to talk to her about this later. "Very well." Handing her child to her mother, Rachel turned and offered Morgan a smile.

He wasn't bad. She just wasn't used to sharing her child with anyone. Not after everything that had happened. She was scared. Things happened. She didn't want to lose Lindsay or hear any more false reports, on her, or true reports for that matter. She didn't want her daughter exposed to any more pain or lies, or to get her hopes up only to have them dashed. She wanted to protect her daughter from the world. And this man was part of that world.

Still, he had been wonderful with Lindsay. If only Lindsay's father had been like that. "It was nice meeting you, Morgan."

Morgan headed toward the door, his long-legged stride taking him gracefully across the room. "I really enjoyed tonight." He pulled open the door and paused, then turned and pierced her with his gaze. "I enjoyed it a lot, Rachel."

Rachel's mouth went dry. "I...yes," she stuttered, and nodded.

"Maybe we'll see each other in church."

The mood was shattered that easily. "I'm not sure. It takes time to get Lindsay ready, and we like to sleep in on Sunday..."

"Oh. I had thought you'd want to take her simply for the interaction with the other children."

"She gets interaction," Rachel argued.

"Ah," Morgan said softly, a smile touching his lips. "But does she get to learn the series of songs the teacher is teaching the children? All of them in sign language?"

"Really?" Rachel asked, excitement burgeoning to life.

Morgan shrugged. "She majored in languages and ministers to the deaf on Saturdays. I thought Lindsay would probably love that."

"She probably would."

Rachel suddenly realized she'd been tricked. Scowling at Morgan, she said, "I only want what's best for my daughter. So if you do see me there, it's because of her."

Morgan's smile turned tender. "I understand, Rachel.'' He reached out and took her hand, but instead of shaking it, to her utter disbelief, he lifted it to his lips and kissed it lightly. His gaze lifted to hers. "I really do." She stared, watching him walk down the stairs and to his car. And for some reason, she really believed that he did understand. She wasn't sure why, but it was in his eyes. The truth. He really did know what she was going through.

Gripping the door, she wondered if maybe, just maybe, God really did take a personal interest, after all.

Chapter Five

She should have known.

He was a doctor.

A pediatrician.

Of all the low-down tricks. She was striding across the green, but she didn't make it to her destination, which was the church day care and her mother. Oh, no. She found someone else to take her frustration out on.

Smiling with grim anticipation, she steered toward the left and the man sitting at a small table under a tree. "Ah, good morning, *Morgan*," she said lightly.

His features changed and lit with a welcoming smile. "Not morning really. I'm on an afternoon lunch break.'' Standing, he smiled, and that smile nearly melted Rachel's anger.

Nearly.

''How are you today? Will you join me?''

So smooth and gentlemanly. It was that kiss on the hand last night that distracted her, made her look at the way his hand waved her to a seat. She found herself moving forward to do just that—when she suddenly jumped back.

''Rachel?'' he asked, confused.

''Don't you take that tone with me. I found out.'' She dropped that bombshell and waited to see him flinch or at least flush guiltily.

He did none of these. He continued to stare at her, looking curious as well as confused. ''Found out what? I'm sorry, Rachel, but I don't understand. Please, take a seat. We can talk.''

Rachel shook her head, her agitation obvious as she clasped her hands. ''Mom put you up to it, didn't she? I just know she did. That's Mom.''

Concern replaced his confusion, and he stepped forward.

She raised a hand to halt him. ''No. Just tell me the truth.'' Silly, but she was near tears. ''She did, didn't she?''

"Rachel, I honestly don't know what you're talking about," Morgan said, and she could tell he meant for her to believe that.

"But…you're a doctor. Mom wouldn't have just invited you over."

"You didn't know I was a doctor?" Morgan asked, surprise spreading across his features. "Oh, Rachel," he whispered, and despite the fact she tried to put up a hand again, he ignored it and pulled her into a gentle embrace. "I just thought your mom had told you something about me since I was a guest there so much."

The strong arms felt nice, encouraging her to lean against him. The chest was wide enough to hold her as she leaned against him. The warm, deep voice invited her to trust him. It was the last that, after only a moment of comfort, made her push back.

"She didn't tell me," Rachel whispered. "You were there to examine my daughter, weren't you?"

He hesitated.

"Don't lie to me," she said.

With a nod, he said, "Your mother wanted me to see Lindsay, but just friend to friend.

She knows you didn't want her to go into an office and see a doctor officially.''

"She doesn't need a doctor," Rachel argued. "She's fine. We're fine. We're both fine.''

Lifting his hands, he said gently, "It's okay, Rachel. I wasn't there to play inquisitor. Believe it or not, I do go over to your mom's house two or three times a week. Sometimes I bring dinner, and sometimes she fixes it.''

"And you sure jumped on it when she asked you to look at my daughter," she said bitterly, feeling raw with betrayal.

"It's not like that. Your mom is worried about both you and your daughter. She loves you, Rachel, and wanted to help. Please don't be angry at her.''

Rachel's shoulders slumped. "I'm not. I'm just—hurt," she finally whispered. And scared, though she didn't add that aloud. She didn't want anyone around her daughter. Lindsay was vulnerable. Rachel was, too. She couldn't take hearing someone else tell her that her daughter was imperfect and should be shut away somewhere.

"Rachel, listen," he began, but the beeper on his belt went off. Looking down, he sighed.

"That's the hospital. I have to take the call. Please, wait on this and think about it. Allow your hurt to ease before you say anything else. We'll talk later. Okay?"

Rachel shrugged. She didn't care what he said. How could her mother have confided in him when she knew Rachel didn't want Lindsay exposed to another doctor?

"Later," he reiterated and then jogged across the lawn toward one of the telephones.

Miserable, Rachel continued across the green to the church, planning to talk to her mother. She hurried up the stairs and into the building.

Before she got very far, Miss Emma stopped her. "Miss White! Oh, Miss White!"

She came bustling toward her, her face wreathed in smiles. "I'm so glad I found you. Can you come in the office a moment? I was filing some church papers and I found some of Lindsay's papers in there. You can take them to your mom for me, if you will."

Rachel sighed at getting waylaid but nodded. "Of course."

Rachel had to admit this woman was certainly a character. She waved her hands and sighed dramatically. "I just don't know how all this paperwork ended up in my office. Papers. Such a mess. Nevertheless, they're much better than putting all that information in those little boxes. I don't trust them. The pastor keeps saying he wants to put one in my office but I tell him, I say, Pastor, you just can't trust them. You put the information in, but what happens if it gets lost in there or what happens if you need it a year later. How do you know what you typed is still in there and didn't get eaten up?''

"Computers?''

"Yes. They're just awful. Such a mess. I keep telling him not to plug in that newfangled instrument but he just can't understand my concerns.''

In her office, Emma moved around her cluttered desk and sat down. "Mind you, now, the pastor is such a good sport. Just single.''

She frowned and started digging through her papers. "Our four-year-old teacher is single, too,'' she informed Rachel.

Rachel smiled politely. "Yes, ma'am. Julianne. I've met her.''

"Of course, you have.'' The woman paused and looked at Rachel, confusion clouding her eyes. "Now what was I looking for?''

"Something about Lindsay to take to my mom."

"Oh! Yes." Emma opened a drawer and pulled out a chart. "Here it is. Lindsay's chart. As I said, I have no idea how that got in here. Your daughter's deaf, isn't she?"

Rachel froze. "Hearing impaired. She can hear a bit."

"Oh, really? I didn't know that was possible. I mean for older people... Is that rain I hear?"

A loud crash of thunder sounded, and Rachel thought, Great, what a perfect addition to the day. She'd be soaked before she got back to City Hall.

"It was cloudy when I crossed the street earlier. I suppose it is rain."

The wind shook the building, and it sounded like a whole flood had been released out there.

"Oh, my," Emma said, her eyes wide. "That sounds like a strong storm."

Rachel nodded. "Yes. I'll just go take this to my mom."

"You do that. Oh, and don't forget to get Lindsay her shots."

Rachel paused in the act of leaving. "What?"

Reverend Ben chose that moment to walk out of his office. She knew he had to be the pastor. He fit the description she'd heard of him.

"Shots. Your daughter's shots are behind. Didn't you know that? They've added new shots to the list of children's inoculations."

"Shots? Now, Miss Emma, I think Rachel here is past the age for booster shots," the pastor teased lightly.

Emma giggled like a schoolgirl. "Shame on you, Reverend. I know that."

He turned to Rachel. "Hello, I'm Ben. You must be Betty's daughter, Rachel. You look just like her."

Rachel smiled politely. "Yes. Thank you. I'm just on my way to see her now." Rachel wondered if someone was trying to block her from going to her mother and yelling at her for doing what she did. Impatient, she smiled shortly. "I really should go."

Rachel felt a drop of water hit her. She reached up, wiped it off and looked at it, hearing Ben say, "Of course. Tell Betty— Watch out!"

Rachel looked up just in time to see Ben lunge for her. Startled, she froze.

The air whooshed out of her when, with a thud, his body knocked into her, knocking her off her feet.

Fear, confusion and pain mixed together as he twisted, trying to keep her from taking the brunt of the fall.

She heard someone cry out and a loud sound like thundering and then another whoosh as water soaked her. Ben rolled with her, coming to a stop against the door with her on the bottom.

Rachel was certain every bone in her body had been rearranged. Dazedly she opened her eyes, to see Ben wince and then scramble off her. "Forgive me, Rachel. Ouch." He rubbed his back. "Are you okay? Here, let me help you." He offered her a hand.

He was soaked, too.

"Wha-what happened?" She wasn't quite sure until she focused on the ceiling. "Where's the roof?"

A big, gaping hole that showed dripping wet pink insulation and silver pieces of paper was where the ceiling once was.

"There," he said, and pointed.

Rachel followed his gaze and gaped. Beams

and insulation and volleyball net and ball lay where she had stood only seconds before.

Realizing Ben still held his hand out, Rachel put her hand in his, and he pulled. She stumbled into him and grabbed her head.

"Emma, is Ben in— What in the world!"

Morgan froze, staring in shock. Rachel looked at him. "You were going to the hospital," she said.

"Dr. Talbot, our roof fell in. Just plumb fell in. It was so awful. You should have seen it." Emma clasped her hands, twisting them with worry. "I've never seen anything like that. Rachel was standing right there and then suddenly Reverend Ben shouted and lunged at her, and they went flying and things started falling and water went everywhere. Oh, my, it was awful."

"You were hurt?" Morgan asked, looking at Rachel.

She was pale and seemed shaken, but other than that, she looked okay. "I—I don't think so. Just a bit dizzy." She rubbed her head.

"Ben, can we use your office?"

"Of course."

"Are you and Emma okay?"

"I'm a bit banged up, but okay. Emma? How about you?"

"Oh, I'm fine. All the papers on my desk aren't. Oh, my, now we're going to have to redo all of this. Anyway, when Rachel's head hit that door, I'd be willing to say she saw stars."

"No, I'm fine, really."

She blushed and pulled back slightly. Obviously, she wasn't the type that liked the attention on her.

"I'm sure you are," Morgan said mildly. "Did your mom tell you your daughter was behind on shots? Oh, and about that call. False alarm. A child that was supposed to be dismissed. They had some questions. I have a new secretary." He explained all this as he cupped her elbow and moved around the pile of debris toward Ben's office.

"Emma. Get a contractor on the phone. I need someone out here to do repair work. Don't worry about those papers now, dear. Just call the contractor. Okay?"

Morgan listened to Ben soothe Emma and smiled slightly. Then Ben was on the other side of Rachel, helping propel her toward his office.

She was unsteady on her feet but coherent. "How old is Lindsay, anyway?" Morgan asked mildly.

"She's three, you know that."

"Ah, yes." He moved her to a chair and seated her.

"Wha— Look, Morgan, I told you I was perfectly fine. I just hit my head."

"Why don't you let me be the judge of that?" he murmured and laid his hands on her shoulders.

She jumped like he'd shot her.

"It's okay, Rachel," he soothed.

"Please, Rachel," Ben said, taking a chair near her. "Let him look you over. You were in the church when this happened, and I want to make sure you're okay. I feel responsible."

"But...but you're a pediatrician!" she cried.

Morgan grinned. "I can give you a lollipop afterward," he said.

He ran his fingers up her neck and felt her stiffen. "It's okay, Rachel. Do you hurt there at all?" he murmured softly.

"No. I'm fine. Do you have any vanilla lollipops?"

Morgan chuckled. "I'm afraid not." Running his fingers into her light brown hair, he worked to keep from being distracted by the soft, shining strands. She was beautiful. There wasn't a thing about her that wasn't attractive. "Here, or here?"

"If you don't have vanilla, why should I let you examine me?" she muttered.

Morgan chuckled. "Because Ben said so, and he's a pastor. You gonna argue with a man of God?"

He felt her chin go up. "I just might if I think he's wrong," she said stubbornly.

Ben smiled. "Good for you, Rachel. Always stand up for what you believe."

Morgan, who had moved to her side, saw the look of disconcertment cross her face. She hadn't expected that answer.

"Ouch!"

"Aha," Morgan murmured.

"Why do doctors always say that after they hurt you?"

"I don't know, maybe to make you think we know what we're doing?"

"Oh, funny, Morgan. Really funny."

"You have a knot the size of Gibraltar on your head here."

"Oh, please, do you realize how big that rock is?"

Again Morgan laughed. "I see you do. Okay, it's not quite the size of an egg."

He squatted in front of her. "Follow my finger, hon. We're almost done here."

All the fight suddenly went out of her. The adrenaline rush was over. "Okay," she whispered.

He moved his finger to the right, the left, in and out. Everything appeared normal. He checked her pupil reaction, which was normal.

"I can't see anything physically wrong, Rachel, but you might let me drive you over to the hospital and have them take an X ray or two so we can make sure."

"No, really." Rachel shook her head then winced. "I just need to talk to my mom and go back to work."

"Work might not be a good idea. I suggest you take the rest of the day off. Then go back tomorrow. I'll write you a doctor's excuse," he said, grinning.

"Wonderful. A pediatrician is writing me an excuse. Reverend Ben, I'm sorry but I really am okay. I'd rather not go to the hospital."

He took her hand. "Are you sure? I'd just hate it if anything was the matter."

Rachel glanced at his hand then nodded. "Thank you for being worried. Maybe I will just take the rest of the day off. Okay?"

That seemed to satisfy Ben. "Okay. If you need anything, please call us here, Rachel. Any of us will be glad to run an errand for you or whatever you might need."

Rachel tilted her head. "You don't know me."

Ben smiled. "That doesn't matter."

She stood, a look of confusion on her face. "I don't go to church."

"Your point?"

"No point," she said. "Thank you."

Morgan decided now would be a good time to break it up. "Let me walk with you down to your mom. That way I can make sure you don't suddenly keel over on me."

The confusion left her face, and she looked at Morgan. "Gee, thanks for the vote of confidence."

Morgan chuckled. "My pleasure."

Ben lifted an eyebrow, and Morgan ignored him. "Thank you, Ben."

"I hope to see you again, Rachel," Ben called.

She thanked him again and left.

Morgan was right by her side. "I swear, someone is trying to keep me from arguing with my mother," Rachel said.

"Did it work?" he asked, helping her around the debris and then walking with her to the stairs.

Rachel sighed. "Yes. I'm no longer ready to yell."

"And all you got out of it was a two-by-four to the head."

"That's not funny," Rachel retorted, but she grinned.

"Sometimes God does have to use a two-by-four to get our attention, which reminds me, Rachel, I'd like to apologize for the misunderstanding earlier. I really didn't know you had no idea I was a doctor."

Rachel paused on the stairs and studied him. "I believe you."

"I'd like to make it up to you, if you'd let me."

"You don't have to. Really."

"I'd like to take you and Lindsay to the new

children's movie musical that's playing in the theater right now.''

Rachel stopped dead, turned and stared at Morgan. ''She's deaf.''

''I know that.''

Slowly she nodded. ''Most people don't think she needs to go to the theater because she can't understand what they're saying.''

''I'm not most people, Rachel. I know deaf people hear in other ways.''

Rachel hesitated, and he saw the last of her wariness fade away. ''You're working hard, Doctor. I wonder why.''

''Maybe because I've found something I want to work hard for,'' he said, and lifted her hand to kiss it.

She gaped at him before swallowing loudly. Oh, she didn't realize she'd done it. But she had. She also did it last night. This woman needed courting. Her husband had been insensitive to the fact that Rachel needed tenderness. And Morgan wanted to be the one to give her that tenderness, including leading her back to her heavenly Father. So much of the pain would leave her eyes if she only found that joy once again.

"Lindsay would love it, so because of that, I accept."

Morgan smiled.

"One thing, though."

"What's that?" he asked.

"Don't ask me if you can examine her, and if you ever hurt her I'll never forgive you. And I'll take it on as my personal quest to make sure you regret it to your dying day."

Morgan didn't take offense. He heard the anger, pain and bitterness in her. Someone had really hurt this woman. His heart ached. "You have my word, Rachel."

"Good." He'd surprised her. Morgan supposed she thought he'd walk away. But he didn't. He wasn't that type of man. When he committed himself, he was there for life, good times and bad times. He wasn't planning on backing down. On this or on helping Rachel find her joy.

Chapter Six

"Are you ready?"

Rachel pulled her head out of her car and smiled. "Hello, Morgan."

Rachel had to wonder why she had agreed to this. She'd been in town three weeks, and suddenly she was taking her daughter to a movie with a stranger. Well, okay, not a stranger, exactly. But why did she get the feeling she had dropped into the middle of a play and didn't know her part? Things were going on all around her, and she was simply being carried along.

It was eerie to feel like this was right where she belonged. She didn't trust the feeling. It could get her in trouble too easily. Make her trust when she shouldn't.

Morgan understood. She didn't know how, but she could see it in his eyes.

"Mo gan!"

Rachel turned to see her daughter pull loose from her mother on the steps and run down, signing at Morgan.

He grinned. "Hi, sweetheart," he signed and said at the same time. "Wanna watch a movie?"

Rachel corrected him. "Like this," she said, and touched her daughter. "Movie. You want to go see a movie with us?"

"I'm afraid to ask what I said instead of movie."

She chuckled. "I'm not sure what it was."

"Yeh!" Lindsay said and threw herself at Morgan's legs.

"I think she's taken to me," Morgan said, grinning as he lifted the little girl into his arms.

"I think so, too."

Oops. Lindsay kissed him and then lunged out of his arms toward her mother. Rachel caught her.

Morgan looked like he was ready to have a heart attack.

"She does that sometimes. She has no fear of falling." Rachel gave her a kiss and put her into the car. "I hope you don't mind me driving. I have her toddler seat in here."

Morgan shook his head. "Not at all. Betty, you mind me leaving my car in the street there?"

Betty leaned against the post. "Not at all. I'm going to mow the lawn while you're gone. So getting in and out of the garage will be easier for me."

"Why don't you leave that for me, Betty?" Morgan complained.

Rachel watched as her mom smiled and laughed. "I'm not helpless, Morgan. Now, go have fun. Lindsay needs this. I'll see you later."

The sky was cloud-free and sunny. The grass was growing, though not a lot. This would be the first time her mom had mowed the lawn this year. All in all, it was a beautiful day.

Lindsay was caught up in pointing out every person they passed and calling out something about them. Rachel drove down the quiet streets. "I want to thank you, Morgan, for suggesting this. Lindsay hasn't slowed down since she found out we were going to the movie. She is thrilled.''

"When's the last time you got to take her?" Morgan asked.

Rachel smiled, though it was a sad smile. She slowed to a stop at the corner and then looked both ways before turning. "Once since her father left us. It's been a while."

"Well, hopefully, since life is slower here in the small city, you'll have more chances."

"City life. It was too hectic."

"I used to be a doctor in the city. I also studied in a large metropolitan area. This is the best decision I made. I only wish I had made it before I started school."

Hearing a note of melancholy in his voice, she glanced at him. "You lost someone, too?"

His gaze snapped to hers. She didn't get to see the full reaction because she had to look at the road. What she did see, though, told her she had hit the nail on the head.

"A slower life gives you time to think, to prioritize your life. Things I didn't do when I was younger."

Rachel nodded. "I'm still trying to do it," she murmured. She turned into the parking lot and parked. Morgan slipped his seat belt off, exited the car and moved around to open her door in the time it took her to turn the engine off, pocket the keys and release her seat belt.

Startled, she smiled at him. "Thank you. Has anyone ever told you that you're very old-fashioned?"

"Is that a complaint?"

"What if it was?" she said, enjoying the banter between them as she opened the door for her daughter. Lindsay was already out of her seat belt and waiting for her to open the childproof door.

"Well, ma'am, I suppose I'd just have to try harder to make you appreciate my gentlemanly manners."

Rachel tossed back her head and laughed. "You would."

"You're beautiful when you laugh, Rachel."

The laughter died. However, before she could comment or even react to what he had said, he turned and headed toward the ticket counter. "I'm buying, I hate to say. Since I invited you out, I'll buy."

Rachel nodded. "Thank you."

"That's better. Accepting the gentlemanly behavior already."

"You're impossible."

"I try. So, Lindsay." He directed his words to her when he managed to get her to gaze at him. "Do you like popcorn?"

She looked at him blankly.

He glanced at Rachel. "I don't think she's ever had it," Rachel offered in explanation.

"What?" Mock outrage shone on his face. "No popcorn? Ever? You have neglected this poor child. We have to have popcorn and lots of it—extra butter."

"That's messy," Rachel said, her mouth twisting in a grimace.

"Doctor's orders," he said smugly.

Rachel chuckled. "Popcorn?"

"But I like it," he added.

"I didn't realize I was taking two kids to the theater," Rachel murmured as they walked into the old-fashioned movie theater.

A grand staircase on each side curved up and around to what was now a second theater but had originally been the balcony. The chandeliers that were anchored from the ceiling had been there when she was a little girl. The red carpet under her feet was threadbare but still the original. However, the walls had changed. Gone was the dark paneling and in its place was light wallpaper. The concession area had changed, and the theater had video games in the lobby.

She grabbed her daughter's hand when Lindsay headed toward one. "No, honey."

Morgan bought popcorn, drinks and a special kid's pack for Lindsay, and they all went in and sat down.

Lindsay crawled into the end chair—why did children always want the end?—forcing Rachel to step over her to sit down. Morgan moved in and sat next to Rachel. "I've heard this movie is really good. Better than the last few."

"Since we haven't seen the last few, I wouldn't know— You go to children's movies?"

Morgan chuckled. The lights were low, which made it feel that much more intimate as his deep laughter wrapped its way around her senses. "You've found out my secret," he whispered. "I'm addicted to G-rated movies."

She giggled. "Are you sure you're a grown-up? Or did a little boy get deposited in that body of yours?"

"Guilty as charged, ma'am."

Lindsay bounced and pointed as the previews came on. Rachel settled back to watch the movie. Morgan offered her some popcorn, and she found herself accepting. In moments the movie started, and they were engrossed. It wasn't ten minutes into the movie, though, that Lindsay gave up her popcorn and drink to crawl in her mom's lap.

Lindsay thoroughly enjoyed the movie, pointing, laughing, and squealing as the hero ended up totally soaked, among other things. Rachel enjoyed watching her daughter.

She hadn't seen Lindsay delight in anything so much in a long time. Before she wanted it to end, the movie was over. Lindsay was exhausted. And everyone was rushing out to their cars. Rachel and Morgan waited for the crowd to thin. "You want me to carry her?" Morgan asked as they stood.

"I'm fine."

"You're stubborn," he replied, and lifted the tired child from Rachel's arms. "She's been on your lap over an hour and a half. Come on, let's get out of here."

"She enjoyed it," Rachel said, not minding that he had taken the burden of Lindsay. At three years old, she was getting heavy.

"So did I," Morgan murmured.

"So did I," Rachel agreed.

"Are you glad you came?" Morgan asked, holding the door open and letting Rachel slip under his arm and out of the theater.

Smiling at him, she said, "Yes. Very much. I don't know when I got so overburdened that I forgot how much my daughter needed to get out occasionally."

"Single parenting is hard, Rachel."

"You don't have to tell me," she muttered as she opened her car door and unlocked Lindsay's door. Morgan set Lindsay into the seat and buckled the belt. He closed the door and held Rachel's door until she was seated.

Then he walked around and slipped into the passenger's seat. "Don't blame yourself," he began after she started the car and headed down the street. "It's just one of those things. You've noted it, now just work to change it."

"But how? Sometimes I think... I just feel I'm going to faint instead of winning the race of getting her to adulthood." She sighed in dismay. She hadn't meant to tell him that. She had to learn not to let things slip like that. All he needed was to hear something stupid and he'd be telling her to put Lindsay in a home immediately.

"I'm not the enemy, Rachel. Believe it or not, I do understand. Sometimes when life is overwhelming you, you feel like a grain of sand in a sandstorm. But we tend to forget what we can't see. God. God is there, on our side, holding our hand. He's not going to let us slip. He'll see us through."

"I don't know about that. I don't really know—" She broke off and shook her head, refusing to tell him her confusion and worry about God.

"Another thing you might consider, Rachel. Most mothers of handicapped children don't take enough time for themselves to relax and get rid of the extra stress raising a challenged child brings. You might want to consider that in the equation, as well."

"I don't have time."

"You didn't," Morgan gently corrected. "You're here in Fairweather now. Take time to relax. Schedule it into your week. On this day I will relax. Make yourself plan something—even if it's just staying around the house in the backyard. Play cards with your mom or get away if the stress is too much."

"I've read the statistics about challenged children and their parents, Doctor. I know all about stress. I know all about the strain of single parenting and the need to spend time with my child and read to her. Shall I go on?''

Morgan chuckled. "Doctor mode again?''

Grinning, she nodded. "Doctor mode.''

"I offer my most humble apologies, fair lady.''

She giggled. "Do you treat your patients this way?''

Morgan leaned back in his seat, enjoying the way Rachel's face glowed when she laughed. Her blue eyes sparkled, and her smile stretched. Her head tilted just so as her hair moved around her face. She was beautiful. And in his heart, he knew she was the woman who was his destiny. Thank you, Father, he silently acknowledged. But what about my past? A small cloud of worry fogged his good mood. That was something he didn't want to think about, let alone discuss.

"Morgan?''

"Huh? Oh. Well, the little girls certainly like my fair-maiden line. The teenage girls, too, for that matter. I don't think the boys would appreciate being called fair lady, though. Gallant knight, brave solider, maybe, but not fair lady.''

Laughter rang out in the car as she turned onto her street. The pleasure was easygoing and companionable until she pulled into the driveway. Morgan opened her door, and Rachel slid out and retrieved her sleeping daughter.

She paused, grinning. "Thank you so much for taking Lindsay to the movie. She really enjoyed herself. Would you like to come in before you go?"

He opened his mouth to answer when two teenage girls skating by, knee pads and safety helmets on, burst into giggles.

"Dr. Morgan's on a date! Ooh, Dr. Morgan has a girlfriend!"

"I know you, Tabitha!" Morgan called, and waved a warning finger at her and the other girl.

He turned back, and that's when he knew there was a problem. Rachel looked pale as a ghost. He looked from her to the girls and back. Understanding dawned. The thought of their time together being called a date, the fact that she had been referred to as his girlfriend, terrified her.

"It wasn't a date," she whispered.

He touched her hand, wrapped around Lindsay's back. "Of course it wasn't. Well, maybe with Lindsay," he joked, trying to ease her dismay.

"The whole town is going to be saying we're dating."

"Oh, I doubt that. Tabitha isn't a gossip. She just enjoys giggling and being silly like all teenagers. Besides, how many teenagers talk to their parents? Furthermore, if you're worried about that, you shouldn't have gone into a dark theater with me," he teased, grinning.

Rachel moaned.

"Come on, Rachel. It's okay. It doesn't matter what others think. Let's just relax and give it time and have fun with Lindsay. Remember, that was what we went for, so she could have fun."

Rachel slowly relaxed. "Yeah. Yeah, you're right." She looked at Morgan and gave him an apologetic smile. "I'm sorry, Morgan. I just have no desire to marry or date or anything like that," she added too hastily, tipping Morgan that marriage was a word she didn't like at all. "I mean, I just got back to town, for Pete's sake. I have a daughter, a new job and I'm trying to get on my feet! I'm still hurting from the betrayals Jim tossed out, and that

Lindsay no longer has a father. I'm just not ready for anything like that.''

''And since you know that and I know that, let's just enjoy the time we have with Lindsay, okay?''

Rachel nodded. ''Yes. That sounds great.''

''Speaking of which,'' he said as he escorted her to the door, ''has Lindsay ever been fishing?''

''Fishing?''

Morgan grinned a boyish grin that almost certainly boded ill for her.

Chapter Seven

Later that evening, Rachel came out of Lindsay's bedroom, stretching tiredly.

"So, how was the movie, honey?" Betty asked, sitting on a sofa in the living room with a hot cup of tea.

Rachel picked up the toys her daughter had scattered as she replied, "I enjoyed it. Lindsay enjoyed it. We had a good time. It was a long day, though."

"Leave those for later. Let's talk. I rarely get much time with you."

Rachel took the toys she had gathered and dropped them in a basket in the corner. She then collapsed on the sofa and stretched out her legs. "I'm exhausted."

"Lindsay is asleep, then?"

"Finally. She really enjoyed herself. I feel bad that I haven't taken her out more often."

"Oh, please, how frequently did you get to go as a child? Lindsay isn't spoiled. I agree the two of you need more free time, but don't beat yourself over it, darling."

Rachel grinned. "You sound like Morgan. He encouraged me to take more time off but not necessarily at the movies. He suggested that just going out in the backyard was fine."

"He's a smart man."

"And a doctor," Rachel added.

"Imagine that," Betty said. "How long have I known him now, and he's a doctor."

"Why'd you do it, Mom? Why'd you go behind my back and invite him over?" Rachel hadn't been able to ask her mom. Her mother had been too busy clucking over her in worry. And they hadn't had any real time to sit down together since.

"Because I was worried for you."

"Me?" That surprised Rachel.

"Yes, you. You are so steeped in hurt and anger over what that ex-husband of yours did. Honey, I wanted a doctor just to look at her, to be able to say, 'no, Rachel, this problem isn't your fault, your marriage falling apart wasn't your fault,' and if there is hope, to say, 'let me look at her and see if there is something we can do'."

"I don't want any doctors examining her," Rachel said firmly.

"Morgan is different. Has he once treated Lindsay as anything other than a three-year-old child? Has he ever said he believed in putting children in homes? Getting rid of them?"

"No."

"Don't get me wrong. I'm sure there are instances, when a child is severely handicapped, the mother must make that decision. Did you know your great-uncle Mitchell was in a home like that? It was a Christian organization, and they treated him well. He died when I was eleven."

"You never told me that, Mom."

"I don't know why. Anyway, though, you know Morgan wouldn't do that. He's not like that idiot doctor that you had back in the city."

"I just don't want her being poked at."

"Think about it, Rachel. I'm not asking you to right now. You have to know the doctor and believe in him before you go. Speaking of which, how is your head? Is the lump finally gone?''

"Yeah, I can even comb my hair without wincing.''

"Good.''

"Have they fixed that hole in the ceiling yet?''

Betty chuckled. "No. And do you know what? We found out today the office ceiling was only a minor problem. I went into the day care, and evidently the water had been running and rotted out two of our major storage areas. It doesn't rain but it pours. Land sakes, the mess. Ben is going to have someone out tomorrow to check on those closets and see about fixing them. Ben's entire time here seems like it has been plagued with problems. Poor boy. He's such a nice man to have all of this happening to him. Morgan is a nice man too, for that matter.''

"How long has Morgan been here?''

"Not very long. I think he has ghosts, though, Rachel. When he first got here there was a look in his eyes. And he was lonely.''

"I saw that look today," Rachel said absently.

"Really?'' Betty looked at her daughter,

surprised. Betty pulled the small coverlet off the back of the couch, wrapped her flannel-clad legs in it and waited for her daughter to elaborate.

"We were talking about him losing someone."

"He told you he'd lost someone?" her mother asked.

"No, I asked him about something he said, and that look crossed his face."

Rachel remembered the haunted look and sighed. "He acts like he really understands Lindsay, Mom. Like he feels her pain, her problem and my pain. It's a little eerie."

"Perhaps God put him in your path for a reason, dear." Shifting, she took a sip of her tea. "Maybe he does understand more than we realize. God has a way of working things out, you know."

"I'm just not sure. I want to believe, Mom, but I just don't know if I can. Too much has happened, too many things. How can I believe God really takes an interest in me, in Lindsay when he allowed her to be born with a problem that eventually made her father leave her, a problem that it's possible I caused her while she was in me? Why would God allow that?"

"You can't blame God for Lindsay's hearing problem, Rachel. Besides, God can always heal her. If he chooses not to, then perhaps there's a reason. You never know whom Lindsay might minister to. I know it's hard, honey."

Betty leaned forward and touched her hand. Rachel took her hand and held it. There was pain in her mother's eyes as she said, "It's really hard to understand when you lose someone and don't understand why. I loved your father dearly. I have no idea why God took him when he did. However, it's something I have to accept and then go on. Trust God with your life, Rachel. Let go of the fear and pain, honey."

Rachel struggled with tears. "I'm trying, Mom. I really am."

Her mother smiled at her. "That's all I can ask of my baby. Now, give me a hug and go get in bed. You're exhausted and need sleep. I'll see you in the morning."

Rachel stood and gave her mother a hug. "You know, Mom, I really love you."

"I know, honey, and I love you. But I never get tired of hearing it." Hugging her daughter tight, Betty gave her a kiss and then shooed her off to bed.

When she was gone, Betty looked up at the ceiling. "She's in your hands, Father. The hardest thing is learning to just accept. I'm trusting You to teach her that lesson."

Returning her attention to the living room, she picked up her book and began to read.

Chapter Eight

"This water is absolutely freezing!"

Morgan chuckled. "Nah, it's brisk. Don't you like it?"

Rachel laughed and shook her head. "My piggy toes are going to fall off."

Lindsay laughed and splashed her bare feet in the water. "Iggy ohs iddy ohs."

"She's really good at imitating what you say. Just how much does she hear?" Morgan asked, and sat on the ground near Lindsay and helped her adjust her miniature pole before tossing his line into the water.

Rachel shrugged, sat and picked up her pole. "I'm not sure. She picks up a lot, though. She has trouble with the beginnings and endings. Diphthongs, things like that.''

Morgan nodded. ''She's a very smart little girl.''

''You don't have to tell me. Did you hear what she did to Jeremy yesterday?''

''Well, let's see, I didn't treat him for a marble up his nose, nor did I treat him for a black eye. What else could it be?''

''It was actually awful. I shouldn't laugh. But my mom said I did the same thing to my brother.''

''Uh-oh. In the genes, is it?''

''I guess. She played barber with him and cut his bangs.''

Morgan chuckled. ''Did you do that, Lindsay?'' he asked the little girl.

She frowned. ''Bad.'' Spanking her hand, she continued. ''Maauu spaen me.''

''Spanked? Hey, I only patted your hands for sneaking the scissors out of the teacher's desk,'' Rachel argued, grinning at her daughter.

Lindsay went back to fishing.

''And yet you did it, too?'' Morgan prompted.

Rachel giggled. ''I got more than a tap on

the fingers, Morgan. Mom said Dad made me go sit and watch my brother get his hair cut and then I had to get my own cut. By the time they were done shaving his hair off—I'd cut it right in the middle on the top—I'd promised never to cut his hair again. I was terrified that they were going to give me the same haircut. I would have much rather had a spanking, I'm sure.''

"Oh, I'm sure," he agreed, chuckling. "Oh, look! Look, Lindsay. You have a fish."

"Oh!" Rachel jumped up and helped her daughter bring it in. Lindsay was so excited she did more harm than good. Morgan wondered how in the world the two didn't lose the fish as they jumped and bounced around while trying to pull it in.

Lindsay squealed with absolute delight when the floppy silver fish hit the sand. "Lemee hol id." She held her hands up to take it. "Oooh boo ee ul…"

Lindsay held it close, touching the pretty colors on its side before wrinkling her nose. "Eeeuwww."

Walking carefully to Morgan, she held it out. "Mine."

"That word certainly came out clearly,"

Morgan said. Grinning at Lindsay, he nodded. "Yours."

"I think she learned that at the day care. I hadn't heard it before that." Rachel set her fishing pole to one side and joined them, admiring the fish with her daughter.

"What do you want me to do, Lindsay?" Morgan asked as Lindsay continued to stand with the fish in her hands.

She shoved the fish at him again.

"I think she wants you to pet it."

"Ah." Reaching out, he stroked the side of the small fish.

Lindsay smiled a perfectly beautiful little smile at him and toddled over to sit on the ground with the fish still in her hands.

"Lindsay, the fish has to stay in water to live." Rachel dumped an icebox that contained picnic supplies and dragged it to the water's edge.

Morgan rose and helped Rachel fill the chest with water, then carried it to where the child sat. "You have to be careful, honey, or you'll hurt it. Put it in the water. Pretty fish. Needs water."

Rachel signed it to her daughter when she hesitated.

"Mine," Lindsay said, and looked forlornly at the fish.

"Yes. It's yours. Put it in the water and play with it." She waited.

Lindsay finally obeyed her mother, though reluctantly. However, as soon as the fish started swimming Lindsay became entranced and was perfectly happy sitting there. She regaled them with every move the fish made. Lindsay sang to the fish, she talked to the fish and she had a thoroughly wonderful time watching the fish swim.

Morgan grinned at Rachel. "Funny what little things interest children, isn't it?"

"It never ceases to amaze me."

"We should take those lessons to heart, see the joy in the little things, take pleasure in the everyday things."

"Is that what you did when you moved here?" Rachel asked.

Morgan paused in the act of reeling in his fishing line. "I try to, Rachel. I do my best to trust God and remember that He made the day. Then I try to simply rejoice and be glad for that day. Of course, that's a lot easier said than done."

"Yeah," Rachel said softly. She realized

sadly the only times she had to relax and enjoy anything lately was when she was out with Morgan or Lindsay. Still, even with them, there was something missing, an emptiness they couldn't fill.

"Shall we eat?"

She grinned at him. "Since neither one of us caught fish to cook?"

"Yeah. I guess Lindsay showed us both up."

He stood and offered Rachel a hand up, then helped set up lunch. They had to coax Lindsay away from the fish. The lure of fruit punch did the trick.

Rachel was glad they had convinced Lindsay to sit with them and eat now, instead of later, when they were fishing. Had she allowed Lindsay to wait, she wouldn't have gotten to eat, because just as they finished lunch, Morgan's beeper went off. He checked the number. "It's the hospital. Let me call and see what's going on."

He went to the car, pulled a cell phone from the pocket of his casual coat and dialed. Rachel watched. He looked so natural in his jeans and pale blue shirt, leaning against the car with his phone to his ear. He was muddy from mid-calf down. But she didn't mind. She was muddy, too. And poor Lindsay—she even had mud in her hair.

Morgan's deep voice echoed quietly as he talked. Rachel enjoyed watching him until the corners of his mouth turned down in a frown. He said something and hung up. He came over and squatted next to Rachel, his arms resting on his bent legs, hands hanging loosely between his knees. "I have an emergency. I'm going to have to go back to town. They're preparing the child for surgery now."

"Oh, dear," Rachel murmured, concerned.

"He'll be okay, I'm sure, but I always go in to be with my kids even if I'm not performing the operation. Bobby was in an auto accident and has a fractured femur."

"Oh, no," Rachel whispered. She couldn't believe he was here in front of her and apologizing for having to go in on an emergency. It touched her, made her realize just what a gentleman Morgan was. "Of course, you have to go. I'll get the remains of lunch if you'll get Lindsay," she said, then paused in shock.

Morgan grinned. "Thanks, Rachel. That trust just now meant a lot to me."

"I—I'm sorry, Morgan. It's hard."

Squeezing her hand briefly, he said, "I know," then stood.

Morgan went over and scooped Lindsay up, eliciting a squeal from her. "Gotta go, munchkin," he said, then signed it.

Rachel turned her attention to quickly cleaning up everything and putting the ice chest into the trunk. When she turned, Morgan was carrying the other chest—still full of water.

"What are you doing?" she asked, shocked.

Lindsay trotted right by him. "She begged me. I couldn't tell her no."

He gave her such a pitiful look, she burst out laughing. "You're a pushover. Did you know that?"

Rachel grinned then turned to her daughter. "In the car, Lindsay. We'll see if Grandma will let us keep the fish."

Lindsay clapped before crawling into the back seat to be with her fish. Rachel strapped her in while Morgan strapped the fish in. Morgan slipped into the driver's seat, since it was his car. When Rachel was strapped in, they took off. They were only ten minutes from town. It took two minutes to reach their house after they hit the city limits. Morgan pulled into the driveway and parked. Quickly and efficiently he pulled out the ice chest, carried it to the porch and set it down.

Turning, he nearly ran into Rachel, who was coming up the stairs. Catching her, he wrapped his arms around her. "Sorry, there," he said, steadying her and Lindsay.

Rachel met his eyes. And it just happened. Neither one planned it. Neither one could have predicted it. She stumbled into him. He caught her and then, as if it were the most natural thing in the world, he slowly leaned forward, drawn by invisible chords of attraction, and kissed her. On the lips. In front of Lindsay, God and anyone walking down the street.

Warmth radiated through her, and happiness, as she realized how much she had missed this part of marriage. This had died so much longer before her actual marriage had.

And this kiss was different. This was gentle, tender, consuming, making her feel special. This kiss gave. It didn't greedily take or demand.

Morgan's arms around her held her lightly, warmly as he kissed her. They weren't harsh or rough but questing, protective, and somehow they even felt nurturing.

Rachel melted into the gentle show of affection and responded.

When he pulled back, he looked as surprised as she felt. He hesitated, then ran a hand over the back of his neck. "Rachel, that's not the way I wanted to do this. But I have to go, so we'll have to talk later." He gave Lindsay a kiss on the forehead and hurried down the stairs toward his car.

"Yes, later," she mumbled, tingling all the way down to her toes and up to the ends of her hair from his kiss. She decided right there it didn't take sticking her finger in an electrical socket to curl her hair. Morgan could do that with a simple kiss. "No. Not later. Wait...no." But it was too late. He was gone. Backing out, turning the car, driving off down the street. "Not later. Remember, Morgan? I said I didn't want to date or get involved!" She knew it was useless to tell him that, as he was gone. But it made her feel better to vent. "If you didn't want to be involved, why did you kiss him back?" she muttered. "Smart, Rachel, real smart."

Her daughter wiggled to get down. Rachel realized she was standing on the porch scolding herself. Worst of all, she was doing it out loud. She groaned.

Lindsay bounced into the house calling for Grandma and begging to keep the fish.

Rachel continued to stand on the steps, staring off to where Morgan had disappeared.

She was certain they were definitely in the fire now. She just wasn't sure if it was a good one or bad one. Lifting her fingers, she touched her lips.

She was certain of one thing, though. Morgan had plans to find out.

Chapter Nine

"Oh, my, a fish. I'm so proud of you, honey. Go wash up. Rachel? We have company. Come on in."

Rachel only then noticed the vehicle parked across the street that didn't belong there. Curious, she climbed the stairs and strolled into the house.

And silently groaned. Her mother's pastor sat in an armchair in their living room. Dressed in jeans and a polo shirt, Ben Hunter grinned. "Hi, there, Rachel."

He stood and strode across the room toward her, his hand outstretched.

Rachel automatically offered her hand in return and then winced when she realized it smelled like fish.

The pastor didn't bat an eyelash. "I see you've been fishing," he murmured, a warm smile curving his lips and lighting his entire face with kindness.

Looking down at her three-quarter-length pants, sloppy blue T-shirt and ratty boat shoes, Rachel thought his comment a vast understatement. She looked more like she'd been used for bait instead of using bait. "Um, yeah, with a three-year-old."

Betty walked in from the other room. "Lindsay wants to sit out on the porch with the fish after she cleans up. I told her it was okay. Ben came by to see how you were feeling, dear."

Rachel shook off the feeling of embarrassment, moved politely into the living room and carefully seated her smelly self in the wooden rocking chair.

"Please, Rachel, if now isn't a good time, I understand. I only wanted to check and see how your head felt."

Now that was certainly a surprise. A pastor making the house calls a doctor once made.

She found herself smiling at the thought. "Quite well, actually. No more pain."

Ben nodded before picking up his cup and taking a sip of the hot orange spiced tea. "Your mom and I were planning the family social. We try to rotate who is in charge, and I asked her if she'd like to do it this month."

Betty, in her khaki pants and red top, the sleeves pushed up, seated herself. "And I said I'd be more than happy. So, how was your fishing expedition?"

Betty sat back and waited attentively for her daughter to answer. Ben waited, too. Rachel suddenly felt as if she were under a microscope. "Good, I suppose. Lindsay had a great time. Morgan enjoyed fishing, though he had to leave on an emergency."

"I hope it wasn't serious," Betty murmured, concerned.

"Surgery," Rachel murmured. "By the way, Lindsay is the only one who caught a fish."

Betty grinned. "Oh, that's wonderful. She certainly is proud of that fish."

"Yeah." Rachel chuckled. "She wanted to carry it around everywhere she went. We had to convince her to leave it in the ice chest. And then Morgan, while I was packing the picnic basket, allowed her to talk him into bringing it home.'' She shook her head in disbelief. ''He's such a pushover with the kids. I don't know how he can perform his job. Surely the kids have his number by now?''

''He's one of the best,'' Ben said quietly.

''Oh, my, yes. All the children at the day care love him,'' Betty added. A chuckle slipped out as she continued. ''They more than love him, they follow him around like he was the Pied Piper.''

Not caring one bit for the turn the conversation was taking, Rachel decided to take charge of its direction and turned her attention to Ben. ''Thank you, Reverend, for stopping by to check on me. I'm a bit surprised you did since I don't attend your church.''

Ben smiled an amiable, fond smile. ''You were injured at the church. And you're Betty's daughter. Besides, I wanted to know how you were doing. I wanted to see for myself that you were okay.''

Not used to such concern or caring, Rachel wondered if he had ulterior motives. His eyes reflected no deceit. His voice sounded perfectly honest.

She forced herself to relax. "Thank you."

"And how is Lindsay doing? I saw her in the day care yesterday. She and a little boy were skipping until, well, the incident." Ben chuckled. "Poor Jeremy."

"She recovered nicely from her punishment. It's forgotten. I think she has taken a liking to Jeremy, though. Kids." Rachel made a wry face at the pastor.

"Yeah. I enjoy watching them. Listen, I wanted to let you know that there were some different activities in the church Lindsay might be interested in. Our children's church teacher happens to know sign language and enjoys teaching songs to the kids in sign language as a continuation of ministry. Also, on Saturdays, if you're ever interested, she has a deaf ministry. She goes to the local park, after gathering up the children with disabilities in the surrounding area, and they have a good time singing songs, learning Bible scripture and just hanging out while the parents get a break."

"Morgan mentioned her to me," Rachel replied thoughtfully.

"Ah. I'm not surprised." Sitting back, he crossed his legs.

Rachel cocked her head in query. Ben shifted. "He loves all kids. I'm sure he'd want to make sure you knew of the programs that might interest Lindsay."

"Ah. Well, yes. He did." She found it odd that the two men she'd met from the church both loved children. Oh, why couldn't Jim have loved children? she wondered silently.

"Also, we do have a support group that meets on Wednesday nights for divorced people. Widows, as well. Actually, it's for anyone who once had a spouse but no longer is considered a couple. They meet to talk, share and discuss problems unique to that situation. You're always welcome."

Rachel could imagine going into a room full of strange singles and thought, No, thanks.

Lindsay chose that moment to come running into the room and up to her grandma. "Um see," she said, and grabbed her grandmother's hand.

Betty stood. "I'll be right back. Come on, honey, let's go. Show me your fish," she said and hurried to the porch with her granddaughter.

Ben looked at Rachel. "Let's be honest now that your mom is gone. I make you uncomfortable, Rachel. I wish I didn't. I'd only like to be here for you as a friend, an ear to listen, a pastor to counsel if you need it."

Rachel, surprised by such forthright honesty, nodded, relaxing. "Thank you for that. But, Reverend," she said, and then hesitated. Deciding honesty should be returned with honesty, she said, "I'm sorry. I just— I'm not sure God even cares anymore. I've failed Him somehow and He's turned His back on me. After all, my marriage was a failure. I tried but failed to keep it together—"

"Oh, Rachel, don't blame yourself. It takes two people to make a marriage work. Three, actually. You, your husband and God." Leaning forward, he said softly, "You know what? God doesn't condemn you, dear."

She shuddered.

Studying her, he added, "He loves you, Rachel." Reaching out, he fingered his Bible, which was on the table in front of him. "He's not going to desert you. I'm sure there is something right around the corner for you that you can't see yet."

"I just don't know if I can believe," she whispered.

"Then ask Him, Rachel, to help you believe."

Rachel trembled at his words. They went straight to her heart. "It hurts to fail. And I'm scared, for Lindsay."

"Yes, Rachel. It does hurt to fail. However, you aren't the only one who has failed. I've failed, too, in many areas. So has your mom. So has Morgan. But do you condemn them?"

"No," Rachel answered quietly.

"Then why think your heavenly Father would condemn you?" Picking up his Bible, he leaned back in his chair and lifted his compassion-filled gaze to hers. "In time that pain will fade and heal. The hardest thing sometimes is to trust God—especially when we don't feel His presence. It's that walking on faith that we just have to do." Ben opened his Bible and fished through it for something before meeting her gaze again. "Ask Him to help you, Rachel. He will. In the meantime, if you want to talk to me, any time, day or night, please call me.''

Ben passed her a card with his number on it.

Betty came back. Rachel panicked, afraid he'd say something to her mother. Instead, he changed the subject to the potluck dinner.

He was certainly different than what she expected. When he finally left, her mother turned to her. ''What do you think?''

She shrugged. ''He's a nice man.''

Betty smiled and squeezed her daughter's hand. ''Yes, he is. And he has been wonderful to me since I lost your dad. He also comes over once or twice a month for dinner.''

''Mother! Do you feed the entire town?''

Betty chuckled. ''No, but you know, that man would be good husband material, if you ask me.''

Rachel groaned. ''Well, I didn't. Now I'm going to go shower and then work on some of the paperwork I brought home. Do you want to put Lindsay down for a nap or do you want me to?''

''Oh, please, let me. I love lying down with her. It's our quiet time on the weekends.''

Rachel nodded. She started toward the stairs, but her mom's voice stopped her.

"Rachel?"

"Yeah, Mom?" She turned.

"It's nice having you home."

Rachel smiled. "It's nice to be home."

She continued up the stairs, thinking how lucky she was to have such a supportive mother.

Chapter Ten

Mothers!

Did every mother ever born on this earth feel it her moral obligation to interfere in her daughter's life?

Rachel shifted Lindsay to her other hip and hurried across the street.

"How did your grandma get me to agree to this? I have rocks for brains. Sneaky is what she is. She waits until I'm vulnerable and then she goes in for the kill."

Rachel shook her head. As she went into the building off the town square, she nodded to the nurse. "Lindsay here has an appointment."

The nurse smiled politely. "Please fill this

out, Mrs. White, and then we'll process her papers.''

Paperwork. More and more paperwork. Rachel looked around for a seat. Lindsay wiggled to get down, then ran to a small area that offered an array of toys and books. She plopped down right in the middle of them and began to play.

The office was nice. Very modern. A large, spacious, carpeted waiting room worked up in pinks, blues and yellows had a semi-enclosed fence about three feet high with toys and books in it, chairs and even a video running in an encased TV.

The rest of the area had larger chairs, plastic potted plants and pictures of different cartoon characters hanging on the wall. Literature and magazines were in a rack near the door leading to the back.

Rachel seated herself and started filling out the paperwork. She'd done this three dozen times in the twin cities when she'd tried to get her daughter treated.

There was no help for Lindsay. And she didn't want to hear bad news again. Yet, here she was…because of her mother.

Looking sympathetically at her daughter,

she could only hope they didn't poke and prod Lindsay any more. Lindsay used to cry every time she saw a doctor's office because she'd been stuck, jabbed and examined until she was terrified to go near anyone in a white coat.

Rachel finished the paperwork and returned it to the nurse, who promptly called their names.

Rachel went over and lifted Lindsay into her arms. "Come on, sweetheart. Let's go see Morgan."

Lindsay's smile collapsed when she saw the uniformed nurse. It didn't matter what color they wore, she recognized the scrubs. Her lower lip trembled, and her arms went around her mother's neck.

Rachel's mouth tightened when those tiny little arms squeezed her so tightly. She rubbed Lindsay's back, humming, softly speaking soothing words.

The walk to the small room seemed like forever. She knew her daughter was going to lose it any minute and throw a hysterical fit. Please, God. Please help me with her, she silently whispered.

"Just let me take her temperature and examine her," the nurse said.

Rachel shook her head. "No. She's fine. This is just for inoculations and a general checkup."

"Ma'am, it's our policy to check."

Rachel smiled. "I know. But I'm afraid that will just have to be bypassed this visit. This is her first time to a doctor after a long absence. Dr. Talbot will agree with me if you go ask him."

She could tell she angered the nurse. But she couldn't surrender her daughter to a stranger. If Morgan didn't agree, then she was out of here with her daughter. She was not going to allow her daughter to have any unnecessary procedures. Guiltily she hugged her little girl. "It's going to be fine, Lindsay. Mama will be here."

"Ome," Lindsay whimpered. She wanted to go home.

"Soon," her mother reassured her. "Soon, my darling little angel."

The door opened, and Morgan strode in, surprise clearly evident. "Rachel? Is Lindsay okay? What's the matter?"

This was the first time Rachel had seen him in a lab coat with a stethoscope. He had tall, wide shoulders and dark hair, and he looked even bigger in that white coat. And so like the many other doctors Lindsay had seen in the past. Had she met him like this, there was no way she would have allowed him to get near her. He looked too much like a doctor. Of course, that was because he was a doctor, but for some reason Rachel didn't think of him like that, but as a tender, caring man who had a sense of humor and liked Lindsay.

"She's fine," Rachel said. "Just terrified. I let my mom talk me into an appointment when we came for the inoculations."

"I'm sorry that she had a bad time with other doctors," he said sympathetically.

She nodded and bounced Lindsay, who sensed a change in the room and whimpered louder.

Morgan frowned as he studied Lindsay. "It's a shame, but some kids have a hard time. Other kids are scared or hurt by a doctor who is insensitive," he murmured. Then he smiled. "I have an idea."

He slipped off his coat and tossed it on the examination table. Then he leaned near Lindsay's ear and whispered, "Buzzzzy beee, zzzz, coming to get you, buzzzzz…" and reached around, grabbing her belly.

She jumped and giggled and launched herself at Morgan.

"Hello there, Lindsay."

He seated himself. "I hear you came to see me."

She looked around the room and whimpered. "No lii o-ur. Baaad."

She signed *doctor* and *bad*. Morgan got the message loud and clear. "I like doctors. Watch this," he whispered, and slipped his stethoscope from around his neck, stuck the ends in his ears and put it to his own chest to check.

Widening his eyes, he said, "Thump, thump, thump."

She giggled.

"What does your heart do?"

He reached out and put her hand over her heart. "Thump-thump, thump-thump. Or is it tick-tock, tick-tock?" He signed clock.

"Ump ump," she repeated.

He slipped the stethoscope quickly to her chest before she could object. "You know, I think you're right. That's not a clock at all."

Her eyes widened, and he grinned before releasing the end of the instrument. "Listen," he whispered. "But don't tell Mommy."

He slipped the earpieces from his ears,

quickly inserted them into Lindsay's ears and let her listen. He wasn't sure if she could pick up the noise, but she must have heard something, because her eyes widened and she smiled.

He let her wiggle down, and then he leaned back in the chair, relaxing slightly. Lindsay ran to her mother to let her listen by putting the small end to her ear.

"That's your examination?" Rachel asked, confused.

"No, I was playing with her. The examination will come soon. So, tell me, Rachel. How are you today?"

"I'm fine."

"Sorry I haven't been back over to see Lindsay. The last two days have been hectic. The young child in the accident—his family and I are friends so I've spent a lot of extra time with them. He developed a postoperative infection this morning, but I think we caught it in time. What did Betty have to say about Lindsay's fish?"

Rachel smiled softly. For some reason his explanation eased tension she hadn't realized was there. Had she been that worried about Morgan Talbot coming around again? "Actually, she loved it. It's still alive on our porch, by the way.''

"Have you thought about getting a fish tank for Lindsay?'' he joked.

Rachel stared at him, thinking that would be a wonderful idea. "No, actually I hadn't. I just didn't even think...."

"She really seems attached to the little thing. Maybe other fish would distract her, and you could get rid of it.''

"I should have words with you about bringing it home in the first place,'' Rachel retorted with mock sternness.

"Rachel.'' Morgan uncrossed his legs and leaned forward in his chair. "I have to ask you now, before I examine Lindsay, is this what you really want? I don't want to continue if you're against this, or doing it just because you feel coerced into it by someone else.''

Rachel shoved her hair behind her ear. Was she being coerced? Did she really not want her daughter examined? So many things had happened in the last year, so many changes. One part of her desired her daughter to be healed above everything else. Yet another part of her was terrified to allow Morgan to examine Lindsay. She sighed wearily. "I don't know,

Morgan. I don't want it because I know there's no hope for her and I don't want her—or me, for that matter—hurt again, but then I do want it, the selfish part of me, because I hope there is something which will be unveiled. The mother in me screams and runs from the room at the fear I see in my baby's eyes every time she goes to the doctor.''

"Not every time," Morgan said softly.

His gaze slid away, and Rachel followed it to her daughter, who had the stethoscope on top of her head and was talking.

Rachel couldn't help but giggle. "Why didn't any other doctor ever try to talk with her first before coming in and examining her?"

"So many children to see and so little time to see them, possibly. Of course, it could be that those doctors were overworked or just burned out. Or maybe they just forget what it's like to be in a situation where you aren't in control and don't know what's going to happen."

"She knows you. Maybe that's the difference."

"Maybe." He stood and moved over to Rachel. "Get up on the table," he said.

Rachel blinked. "Excuse me?"

He chuckled, and Rachel noted tiny crinkles around the corners of his eyes when he smiled. The man was too handsome by half. She could spend hours just staring at him and watching all the different expressions that crossed his face, mentally tracing every line on his features and listening to his deep, musical laughter. "Time for your examination. Surely you don't expect your daughter to be examined if you aren't?"

He saw the moment she understood what he was up to.

"Oh." Flushing, she nodded. "I didn't.... Ingenious," she finally conceded.

She hopped onto the tiny pediatric table.

"Did I mention you look nice in your navy suit?"

Her color inched up a notch. "Thank you, Doctor."

He chuckled low. "Lift your arm."

She lifted her arm.

"Now drop it."

She dropped it. "Why?"

"I just wanted to see if you'd do it."

She smacked his arm. He chuckled, and so did she.

He picked up the hammer and walked to her. "Let's check your reflexes."

Rachel paused and looked at her daughter. "Morgan is checking Mommy."

Morgan could tell Lindsay didn't like that a bit, though he never looked directly at her. Still, he could see from his peripheral vision that she frowned and inched closer to her mom's leg.

"Watch this, Lindsay," he said loudly. He moved to Rachel's side where Lindsay could clearly see him. Then, not certain she had heard him, he reached down and touched Lindsay's chin to get her attention. "Watch this," he repeated.

He lifted the hammer, positioned it and tapped Rachel's leg.

Rachel kicked him.

Morgan jumped back. "Good reflexes. Not used to having adults up here," he said, chuckling.

Rachel laughed, too.

Morgan grinned when he heard Lindsay giggle.

"Sit by Mommy and watch," he coaxed, then carefully scooped her up and deposited her next to Rachel before turning his attention away from her.

"Next leg," he murmured. "Anyone ever tell you, lovely lady, that your legs don't quit?"

"Doctor!"

He grinned. "That wasn't a doctor comment, that was all Morgan, Rachel."

He reached out and tapped her leg. Her response was the same.

Lindsay giggled. He handed the hammer to Lindsay and helped her hit her mom's knee, then he helped Lindsay test her knees. Finally, he took the hammer and tried it.

Of course, she had to use it on him, too.

He listened to hearts and poked tummies, looked in ears and examined mouths and eyes. He did rudimentary testing of her hearing and after a lengthy exam he sat down. "I'd really like to test her hearing at the hospital in a little room we have set up especially for testing children's auditory levels. I think her range is more than either one of us realizes. There's something about the way she reacts. You think she might be up to going?"

He saw the fear in Rachel's eyes as she gazed at her daughter. He couldn't blame her.

It was scary when a person was being asked to trust the very organization that betrayed her and her child in the first place. He understood that and hurt for her.

"I—I don't know, Morgan. I won't put her in an institution. Never. Ever," she said emphatically.

Surprised, Morgan assured her, "Never, Rachel. She is quite capable of being in your household."

"She means everything to me. I won't give her up. No matter what."

Morgan realized a whole lot more was going on here than he knew about. "Slow down, honey. Why don't you explain what you're talking about."

Lindsay went over to the children's chalkboard while waiting for the doctor and started drawing.

Rachel glanced at her daughter and then to him. Twisting her hands, she finally said, "Rachel was born after a long labor. I had... problems. We didn't notice her hearing problem at first. She fussed a lot, talked a lot, too. I'm not really sure when I realized she had a hearing problem."

She glanced up. "Actually, I think my hus-

band noticed it first. He—he said she acted…''
She took a deep breath—for courage, he was
certain. Morgan wanted to go over and comfort
her but knew better. He gave her time. It paid
off. She finally said what was so very painful
for her to articulate. ''He said she acted stupid.''

Anger flushed Morgan's face red. He felt it.
Heat surged up his neck into his cheeks and
forehead. ''He called her stupid?''

She shook her head. ''No, she acted stupid.
He thought she was…'' She waved her hands
helplessly. ''He called her retarded, too, and
slow.''

''She's not.''

''I know she's not,'' Rachel returned firmly,
but her voice trembled, indicating just how
much those words had hurt her. What could he
do to help her? He felt helpless as he stood
there watching her pain.

Rachel glanced worriedly at her daughter.
Then he watched her valiant effort as she
slowly worked to bring her emotions under
control. ''Things started deteriorating between
my husband and me. He blamed…'' She nodded toward Lindsay. ''I wanted to prove there

was nothing the matter, that we shouldn't send her away, that we should just love her."

Morgan felt his stomach turn over at her words. Betty had mentioned some things. But he'd learned in his field that sometimes grandparents were wrong. Even parents saw things skewed. But to hear both of them, and Rachel's details added in. They were words so familiar to him that they terrified him. Oh, Father, he silently entreated. It was a plea for help.

"So, you took her to a doctor?" he asked, feeling light-headed. Trying to appear nonchalant, he moved closer to Rachel and stood near the counter. Carefully he put on his professional face to mask his feelings.

"I took her to a pediatrician, yes. He said there was nothing wrong unless something had happened when I had trouble birthing her. He suggested the oxygen supply could have been cut off and made her slower than her age."

Morgan leaned against the counter and listened tight-lipped. "That didn't stop you?"

"I took her to another family doctor who said she had attention deficit disorder."

"ADD..." He shook his head. "Go on." Morgan thought if there was any faddish disease that had been overdiagnosed, that was one that certainly had. From what she said, the doctor hadn't even run tests on Lindsay.

"Another doctor told me it was too early to really tell if there was a problem."

Morgan nodded. "Some feel that way."

Rachel twisted her hands together, though Morgan was willing to bet she didn't realize she was giving her emotions away or she would immediately stop. "My husband wasn't coming home at all, spending his free time away by this period of our relationship. He had mentioned that he'd told his friend about my daughter. His friend was a pediatric doctor who had a sterling reputation for being the best. I thought I'd take her to that doctor. Jim insisted this doctor understood our plight. I misinterpreted my husband, though. The doctor understood my *husband's* plight, not *our* plight. He examined Lindsay and said she had a degenerative disease of the nerves in the ears and that she'd soon be completely deaf and I should put her in a home. He said she would be useless to society because the degeneration of the nerves would spread and she'd end up an invalid. It wasn't right to inflict her on a husband who was doing his best to keep his family together, he informed me.''

Morgan wanted to strangle the doctor. He didn't dare ask the name of the associate, not in his current mood. No, instead he prayed for patience. Quickly, so he could help Rachel. When he felt peace flood him, he finally spoke. "You're hiding her because he suggested a home?"

"Not hiding her," Rachel objected. "Just— well, there's no reason to go back to anyone. I mean…"

She trailed off.

Morgan stood, moved forward and took her hands. "Listen, honey. That doctor sounds like a fool. He could be right. Then again, he could be wrong. You think about it, pray about it and let me know. After all you've told me, I'd really like to examine her thoroughly. I can't give you hope. But then again, I can't say that doctor is right, either. Did he do a CAT scan or an MRI? Any tests at all?"

Confused, she shook her head. "He drew some blood. They all drew blood. Then he put earphones on her head and a couple of other things, like making her identify pictures. Cat, dog, things like that."

Morgan sighed wearily. "He couldn't have possibly..." He broke off. No reason to call the fool a fool in front of her and add fuel to the fire. It was in the past, and he'd just have to concentrate on not letting something like this happen in the future to Rachel or to Lindsay. "Just think about it. Okay?"

Lindsay came running and patted Morgan's legs, covering him with chalk as she babbled incoherently to him.

Rachel glanced at his dark pleated pants in dismay. "Oh, dear."

"Don't worry about it," he reassured her. "I work with kids all day. Promise me you'll think about what I said, instead?"

She hesitated, torn. He ached as he watched her. Finally, however, she nodded. Relieved, he smiled. "Good girl."

"What about her?" Rachel made the motion of giving a shot.

"Tell you what, if you decide to go through with the tests, we'll do them then. But since this is her first visit here, I don't want to do that to her. I'll talk to the day care and see if we can put them off another week."

She nodded. "Thank you, Morgan."

Looking at his watch, he said, "Will you

meet me for lunch in front of the church in an hour? I'd like to treat you to a super-duper all-beef polly dog.''

"I'm afraid to ask," Rachel said, laughing.

"It's a special hot dog the little café near the church offers. Actually, if you don't want that, I'll be crushed, but I'll accept it.''

She smiled. "I'd like to see that, so I guess I'll have to meet you.''

"You wound me, fair maiden," he whispered, covering his heart. She chuckled again and Morgan helped her off the table. She went to her daughter.

"Tell me, are you sorry for coming?''

Rachel paused, her daughter in her arms. "Honestly, Morgan?'' She studied him a moment, her eyes aching with apology. "I don't know yet.''

He was a bit disappointed when she said that, but when she stopped at the door and turned, his hopes brightened. "But looking at it as of this moment, no, I'm not.''

She left.

Morgan waved goodbye to Lindsay. He wasn't sure, but he thought he'd just seen Rachel take another large step in letting go of her past and restoring some of her joy. Silently, he prayed that God would continue to work on her heart and give her the peace that came only from Him, and to lift those burdens she carried.

His nurse stuck her head in the door, looking quite irritated. "Doctor! The patients are backing up!"

"Playtime is over. Back to the grind," he murmured.

"Doctor?" his nurse asked, confusion darkening her eyes.

He shook his head. "Nothing." How could he explain to her how he'd felt just being in the same room with his future wife and child? Especially when his future wife and child didn't know they were his future *anything* yet.

Chapter Eleven

Morgan met Rachel for lunch. It was easy to spot her in that blue suit, her hair pulled back. She looked more professional than anyone else in the area. Striding over, he smiled. "Ready?"

"Fearful anticipation," she agreed.

He slipped his hand to her back and steered her in the right direction. "How's your work at City Hall coming?"

Rachel nodded to someone who waved. "Almost done. Then I have to find another job. Their files were a disaster. I have no idea how they found anything or how their planning commissions... Well, you don't want to hear that. Suffice it to say that going over all their books was certainly time-consuming. I'm actually hoping I can do another job for them in the same area, or that this one will turn permanent. It has nice hours and they're not real strict about me checking up on my daughter.''

"It sounds like you found a good job then.''

"Did things slow down at your office any?'' Rachel queried as she allowed herself to be led into the tiny café.

"Actually, they did. I had two cancellations, so everything worked out just fine. Let's grab that booth,'' he said, pointing to one by the window, "before someone else nabs it. It can be rough in here during lunchtime.''

Rachel chuckled. "Oh?''

Grinning at her, he said, "You have to fight them for tables. It certainly isn't a pretty sight trying to get a little old lady out of your booth. Especially if she's carrying one of those old-fashioned purses that leaves dents in your head.''

Rachel sighed with mock exasperation and slipped into the booth. She snagged a menu and started perusing it. "Poor women of Fairweather. None of them are safe.''

"Or at least, one of them isn't.''

Rachel's gaze shot up at the low, intimate tone, and she found the doctor's eyes locked with hers. She swallowed—twice.

"May I help you?"

Rachel was actually quite happy to see the waitress. Well, she was more than quite happy. She thought of the waitress as a life preserver tossed to a drowning person. Now all she had to do was get her rioting emotions under control.

"I'd like tea and..." Glancing at the menu, she tried to read but couldn't make out a word for the life of her. That look Morgan had given her had shocked her right down to her toes. He was interested in her. She was certain of it. But what was worse—she reciprocated his interest. She couldn't! But she did.

"Yes?" the waitress asked.

"Polly dog," she replied.

Morgan chuckled. "I'll have the number three special. Why don't you bring her that, too?"

"Morgan, I am capable of ordering my own food," she said.

"Sweetheart, there is no polly dog on the menu."

The waitress wrote down the orders and left.

Rachel turned twenty shades of red.

"It's okay. The number three is the special I was teasing you about."

"I just couldn't decide," Rachel said.

"You haven't been here before?"

"I usually eat my lunch at the little table out there. I bring it with me in a bag."

"I do that a lot. Especially now that it's warming up. It's so beautiful right now, everything springing to life. The flowers, both the wildflowers and the planted ones. And it's peaceful. There are a lot of children running around but…" He shrugged. "They don't really bother me."

"School break soon, and then it'll be really hectic."

Morgan agreed. "Unfortunately. Seems there are always more injuries during the summertime."

The waitress returned with the tea and plates. Rachel showed her surprise. "That was fast."

"Fast food. How hard is it to fix hot dogs and fries?"

"True. What is on this?" she asked, turning the hot dog first one way and then the other.

"Sauerkraut, chili, relish, mustard, onions and cheese."

"Oh, dear, I feel heartburn coming on already."

"Or hardening of the arteries?" he asked mildly.

"At least. This is a crime against the taste buds." Still, when she lifted the bun to her mouth and took a bite, she found it amazingly good.

Morgan grinned, gave her one of those I-told-you-so looks, and then bit into his own chili dog.

Rachel chewed thoroughly and swallowed before taking another bite. She really wished Morgan had waited until she swallowed that bite before his next statement.

"So, is this our first official date?"

Rachel choked. Covering her mouth with her napkin, she coughed, her eyes watering.

"You okay?" Morgan asked, leaning forward, concerned.

No! You almost gave me a heart attack with that question. "Yes. Yes, I am." She wheezed the words out. "Just a moment." She lifted her tea and took a long sip.

When the tears cleared from her eyes, she smiled at Morgan a bit nervously.

"Tell me, Rachel, what's on your mind?" His voice ran over her, filling her with warmth and ease.

"Morgan..." she began, then paused. "I don't know how to say this...." She tried again.

"You were married before and are gun-shy?"

Surprised, she met his understanding gaze. "Yes," she replied. "How'd you know?"

Without breaking eye contact, he replied, "Because at one time, I was married, too."

"I didn't know that." Why hadn't her mother told her that?

"No one here does, except Ben."

Ah, well, that explained it.

"It's not something I care to discuss."

She nodded, still adjusting to what he had just said to her. "I understand." Trying to put a form of normalcy on their lunchtime, she started on her fries.

"But I want you to know about it."

She was back to worrying. "Do you really think you should tell me?"

Morgan reached out and captured her hand.

Warmth spread from that small, reassuring touch all the way up her arm, then through her entire body. "Tell me, Rachel, that you don't feel something when I touch you? Tell me what I'm feeling isn't reciprocated? I'm not trying to push you, but tell me, Rachel, tell me that you haven't found we have things in common that you haven't found in anyone else you've met?"

Rachel's mouth went dry. "I—I'm not sure."

He conceded that with a tiny nod of his head. Then he continued. "I'd like to get to know you better. I enjoy spending time with you and Lindsay, and I'd like to spend more time with you. But I don't want to do that without asking your permission first."

"Huh?" She blinked. She knew she hadn't just been asked permission to date her.

Morgan grinned. "I'm very old-fashioned. I just asked you for permission to ask you out on dates and stop by your house."

"I—I..."

Morgan chuckled. "Is it really that hard, Rachel?"

With a loud sigh she slumped in the booth. "You don't do anything normally, do you,

Morgan? I feel like I've just been transported back to some Victorian era or something.''

"You don't like it?" he teased.

"The minute you start telling me the woman's place is in the home, I'm outta here."

Squeezing her hand, the hand she didn't realize he still held, he said, "Never."

Removing her hand from his, she went back to eating.

"Well, fair lady?" he asked.

She studied him. "I...have enjoyed your company this last week. However, I'm just not sure if I'm ready for more."

"I can understand that, Rachel. Why don't we take this at your speed. Feel free to say no whenever you want and to warn me if I'm doing anything that makes you feel the least bit pressured or uncomfortable."

"I'm not looking for a date."

He smiled his understanding smile at Rachel, and her resistance melted.

"Okay," she suddenly said. "If we keep it simple. I mean, at least then my mom wouldn't be looking at me with matchmaking in her eyes."

"Your mom is a matchmaker?" Surprise twinkled in his eyes.

He chuckled. "That's Emma." Glancing at her cup he asked, "Are you done here?"

She took another sip of tea and nodded. "I want to check on Lindsay before I go back to work."

"Mind if I walk along? I'd like to check Chrissy. She's just getting over a cold. I thought I'd take a quick peek on my way back to work."

Rachel relaxed. "Not at all." She'd been terrified when she had agreed that Morgan would—what? Turn into a boogeyman? So anticlimactic. He went on as if nothing had changed. Perhaps it was her. She was the one changing. She was the one adjusting to the idea of actually dating again. She was the one who suddenly was seeing life in a whole new way, one with a future, one with more than simply her striving to make ends meet with only dark, bleak clouds on the horizon.

Looking at him, she couldn't deny she was attracted. But it was more than just his looks. He was a gentleman. He had a sense of humor. He was kind, caring and gentle. She could go on and on.

And he loved Lindsay. Or, at least, he acted like he did.

He paid the bill and they left. She didn't mind when his hand slipped to her back to guide her around different obstacles. Instead, she enjoyed his touch, thinking how nice it was to have someone who was so gentle.

"Did your wife… Did she die?" she asked softly as they strolled down the sidewalk.

Morgan thought, If you only knew. "Yeah. It's been a few years. Right after I started medical school." And that wasn't a lie. She had died, later. Her and her second husband. "Anyway, it was very hard for a while and there are times I wish I could go back—but we just have to accept and go on and lean on God during the times when it's getting to you."

"I wish," Rachel began, "I wish I understood why it all happened."

"Sometimes we don't, until later."

As they started up the steps of the church, Morgan noticed a van pull alongside the curb.

"Hello, Warren," he called to the man who climbed out of the van.

Warren was in his fifties and Rachel noted his short, military haircut, rounded stomach and bright red suspenders holding up his pants.

Santa Claus in the military is what he reminded her of. No beard, mustache or white hair, but otherwise a dead ringer.

Walking up to where he and Rachel stood, Warren nodded. "Howdy, Morgan. You hear they just discovered the damage goes on down into the day care?"

"No, I hadn't."

Rachel nodded. "Yes. It made a mess of two different supply closets. Mom said they're going to put on a new roof, too."

"Yeah. They need it. So can you direct me to a Mrs. Anderson?"

"That's my mom," Rachel replied politely.

"Did I hear my name?" Betty walked up, wearing jeans, an oversize shirt with the sleeves rolled up and looking like Rachel had always pictured her mom—except that her mom was eyeing Warren oddly.

"Mom, this is Warren Sinclair. He's here to work on the day care."

Glancing at Warren she noticed he was giving her mother the same look, one of—*interest!* It quickly passed, but Rachel was almost certain that was what she'd seen.

"It's about time," Betty said. "I am so glad you're here. I've been cleaning out those storage areas all morning. Ben can tell you exactly what is going on, but if you want, Mr. Sinclair, I'll be glad to show you the damage downstairs until Ben gets back from lunch.''

"Warren, ma'am. And yes, thank you, I'd like to see that.''

"Please, call me Betty. Right this way, Warren.''

Her mother led the man off with a short wave over her shoulder at Rachel. Rachel shook her head, certain she was imagining things. "I should go check on my daughter now.''

"Oh, Rachel?''

She glanced at her mom. Both she and the repairman stood near the stairs. Her mom looked perfectly normal now. She'd been imagining that interest, after all. "Yes, Mom?''

"Family day is this Sunday. Ask Morgan what it entails and please do come. I'll call you later about Lindsay's appointment.''

"Okay, Mom.''

"Be careful going down those steps, Betty,'' she heard Warren say. She frowned as she watched them descend out of sight.

"Family day,'' she muttered.

"Once a month we get together. It's fun. We have a day of fellowship. Play games, eat, chat, sing. A bit of everything. Ball, badminton, things like that," Morgan said.

"Really? Mom never mentioned it before."

"It's something Ben started."

"Ah, well, it certainly sounds like fun."

"It is. It's also nice, a way to get to know other people. Sometimes in church, there isn't enough time. This is a way to slow down and just enjoy the day. It'd be nice to see you there, Rachel."

Rachel nodded. "Maybe I'll come."

They went through the church to the day care. Rachel had a moment with her daughter while Morgan checked out Chrissy.

She was surprised to find her mom upstairs talking to Warren, who was walking out the door. She paused to speak with her mom.

"How'd the appointment go?" Betty asked.

"Okay. He didn't do much today. She didn't cry. Morgan was wonderful with her. He asked me if I'd consider letting him run some more tests."

"And what did you say, honey?"

Her mother's concerned tone touched her. "I told him I'd think about it."

Betty nodded. "It's always good to consider things instead of giving an immediate answer."

"I'm just unsure."

"It's okay, honey. You'll decide when the time's right. I know I've interfered more than I normally do, Rachel, and I'm about to do it again. Don't let what your ex-husband did to you affect this decision now. Morgan is a good man. He's good at his job. You can trust him."

"I'm just not sure if I'm ready, Mom. I'm taking it one step at a time."

Betty smiled and touched her daughter's cheek. "I'm proud of you, honey. Whether you realize it or not, I'm very proud of how you turned out and for how strong you are."

Rachel hugged her mom. "I get it from both you and Dad."

She chuckled. "No, you get your stubbornness from your dad and your hesitation, too. Me, I'm strong-willed and tend to go for what I want."

"You, Mom? Never!" Rachel teased.

"Go on, get out of here," her mother said, laughing. "I have work to do, and so do you. Obviously if you have time to insult your mother."

Rachel grinned. "Love you, Mom. See you tonight."

"And church?" she asked as Rachel started out of the church.

She turned, the grin still in place. "Yes, Mom, and church. You've convinced me. I'll come sit through the service if it'll please you. After all, how hard can it be?"

Chapter Twelve

~&~

Really hard, Rachel thought now, shifting uncomfortably as she listened to the people
around her. She didn't know most of these
people. Listening to them talk, though, she realized one reason she'd stopped coming.
Church had become simply a ritual to do every
Sunday morning, Sunday night and Wednesday night. Just like one woman she heard talking about. The woman wasn't talking about the
love of Jesus or fellowshipping of the saints;
instead she was simply speaking of the different committees and when the meetings were.
No mention of the joy to be there, to finally
have time to just be with other believers and

share praise in one voice. She'd been just like that.

She'd lost that first love, she realized. Suddenly a woman's voice caught her attention, and she leaned toward the left to hear what she was saying.

"—I agree that the Reverend has instituted too many things. Land sakes alive, wanting us to cook and then play ball in pants! On church property. Can you imagine?"

Another voice replied, "Young generation. No respect for traditions. Our old pastor never would have done such a thing. It's really a shame, too."

"Caught you," a voice whispered near her.

Rachel nearly jumped over the pew, Morgan startled her so badly.

"You scared me."

"You were eavesdropping," he countered.

"I was—"

"Eavesdropping," he reiterated.

"Guilty," she admitted ruefully. "So, what are you going to do about it since I've gotten caught in my awful deed?"

"Well," Morgan said, grinning, "first, I'm

going to ask you to allow me to sit here with you and your mom during service."

Rachel shrugged. "We don't own the pews."

He dropped down on the pew next to her. "Secondly, I'm going to insist you allow me to sit with you and your mom during lunch. I have to keep all those matchmaking mamas away, you see. A doctor is considered a good catch here in Fairweather."

Rachel laughed, horrified. "You are awful."

"I'm telling the truth," he said, grinning, and then winked at her.

Ruefully, she shook her head. "Ever heard the saying liars are fryers?"

"Don't believe I have, ma'am. Why don't you take time to explain it to me, after church?"

His tone turned soft, and his gaze direct as he said that. Rachel couldn't help but respond. "You have yourself a deal," she murmured.

"Good," he replied.

Betty chose that minute to join them. Rachel turned her attention forward just as the music started.

The songs were beautiful, some fast-paced,

others gentle and slow, but all with one common thread, lifting up your voice in praise to God.

Songs that lifted up, that didn't tear down, that reaffirmed what Christianity was really about. Amazingly enough, Rachel found she enjoyed the song service and relaxed as they sang.

When Ben got up to preach, though, she shifted uncomfortably over the message. It was entitled ''God's Timing'' and he spoke about finding out things in God's own time. Not to try to put Him on our timetable but to remember we are on His timetable, a timetable that doesn't even operate the same as ours, in all probability.

Rachel knew that message applied to her heart. Still, she fought it. She was afraid to really believe that God hadn't forgotten them. Because if she did believe that and then it turned out false, she didn't think she could cope with the disappointment.

Please, God, she prayed silently, *just hold on to us because I can't hold on to you right now.*

The service ended, and everyone stood and

mingled. Women drifted off to set up the food. Men grabbed tables and moved them outside on the lawn. Women and men alike changed into jeans and T-shirts.

Fifteen minutes later everything was ready, and their pastor said the blessing. Before she had said amen, Morgan was at her side. "Go through the line with me?"

"But Mom…"

"Is with Warren," he replied and nodded across the lawn.

Rachel looked disconcerted. "But why?" she asked, unable to stop the question.

"I'd say a romance is brewing," Morgan whispered, leading her and Lindsay toward the food.

"But she's—she's—"

"A widow who still has many good years left in her and just might be lonely for company," Morgan said.

Rachel balked. "Oh, I don't like to think of my mom that way," she whispered.

Morgan threw back his head and laughed, a deep, rich sound that traveled over her in gentle waves. "And can you imagine in thirty years your own daughter saying that about you?''

Rachel had to laugh. ''Yeah. I suppose so. It's just, I've never thought of her with anyone except Dad.''

''Well, start thinking. Even if she isn't interested in Warren, she just might be in someone else.''

Rachel watched her mom and finally had to admit, yes, it was possible. Her mother just might be interested. And she found she was happy for her mom, once she got over the shock.

''So, are my two favorite ladies ready to eat?'' Morgan asked.

''I am. What about you, Lindsay?''

''Um unry, too.''

''Me, too, sweetheart,'' Morgan said. ''I'm starving. Let's go.''

Rachel, feeling better than she had in weeks, followed Morgan. As they got their food she commented, ''You'd think there was a rivalry going on here. Look at those people over there, arguing.''

She pointed to two different groups varying in ages from kids to adults. They were ribbing each other, egging each other on. She'd never seen anything quite like it.

Morgan's chuckle drew her attention. "What?"

"Honey, you haven't seen anything. Wait until after dinner."

"What happens then?"

"Just you wait."

Rachel wasn't sure she wanted to find out what he meant.

Chapter Thirteen

"Umph," Rachel grunted, hitting the ground hard as she was knocked down at first base.

The young boy on first had stepped into the way.

"You did that on purpose. Move that foot. She was safe!"

Rachel rolled over to look up at the coach—who had just yelled—her mother.

"She was not. I got her before." The young boy argued good-naturedly.

"Oh, be quiet, Jason," Betty growled. "I saw it."

Rachel sat up and brushed the dirt off her top.

"Don't let her get away with it, Jason," Ben called, chuckling.

"Don't worry, Rev, I won't," the young boy replied.

"Hey, does anyone mind if I say I was safe?" Rachel muttered.

"No," they both said to her, and burst into laughter.

"Jason, if you don't say she's safe I'll make sure not to fix any more treats for the basketball practices, which will be starting back up pretty soon."

"Betty!" Ben called, aggrieved. "Don't listen to her, Jason," he warned. "Don't let her get to you! Steady now…"

Jason shrugged. "What can I do?" With a roll of his eyes, he said, "Okay, okay, she was safe."

"That's more like it. Get up and dust off, Rachel."

"I didn't know you enjoyed sports, Mom," Rachel said, standing and obediently dusting off. "And I was safe," she said to the young boy.

He smiled crookedly and turned his attention to home.

Her attention turned to the next batter.

"Of course I like sports, Rachel. How many years did your father watch them?" Betty said.

"But you didn't."

"I never had time. I do now," her mother replied, smiling at her daughter. "Come on, let's see a good one from the pitcher," she called.

Rachel chuckled. Most of the church folks had changed into jeans and T-shirts, and she knew why. Yes, indeed. They had to get all that being nice to each other out of their system by trying to kill each other on the ball field.

She had to grin as she thought about it. Old and young, age didn't matter. They adjusted the pitch for the children and were more outrageous with the ones they were closer to. The illegal moves she'd witnessed had scandalized her until she realized that the game was evidently all in fun.

She'd really gotten a kick when the infielders couldn't seem to get the ball that ten-year-old Melody had hit and kept tripping over each other.

Betty hadn't been given too much of a break until she warned them to remember that if she was too sore she couldn't care for their kids.

Of course, Morgan had coerced Rachel into getting into the game, and then she'd found out he was on the opposite team. Egging his pitcher to show her no mercy, he had enjoyed every minute of her shock, laughing his fool head off. He was on third base now. If she made it around there, she was going to have words with him.

The crack of the bat sent her gaze to the batter.

"Rachel! Run, girl!" Her mom yelled it hopping up and down.

Rachel took off, realizing she hadn't been paying attention. The man running to first had hit it long. She ran for all she was worth.

And made it! The older woman at second base was slow responding with the ball. She turned and looked at Rachel before tossing to first.

Morgan yelled from his position. "What'd you do? Block Maggie's view?" She couldn't resist. She thumbed her nose at him. "You know better!"

He threw back his head and laughed.

She imitated him.

Several people on the sidelines hooted and

called mock insults at Morgan for picking on a woman and a guest.

Rachel preened.

A shout went up, and several people, including Morgan, started running toward her.

Startled, she stepped back. She opened her mouth to say something, what, she wasn't sure, but she never got the chance. Something hit her from behind.

She fell down hard, and a body had crashed hard on top of her. Then it registered it must have been the woman who had been playing the base. Heads cracked. Rachel saw stars.

"Maggie! Rachel! Are you okay?"

Ben's voice sounded, along with Morgan's. She heard others she didn't recognize, all talking, querying them. Rachel's ears rang. The other woman moaned and rolled off her.

Rachel rotated the opposite way and sat. Maggie was trying to get up. Morgan wouldn't let her. "Take it easy. Slowly. Too much activity after a slow winter," he murmured. "Let me make sure that's all it is."

"I don't need help," Maggie said.

"Come on now, Maggie, honey, just let me check you out."

Hands reached down and assisted Rachel to

her feet. Several people she didn't know, one or two she did.

"I'm fine," Maggie said as she shrugged off everyone who offered help.

"Maggie, honey?" Frank shoved through the people to his wife's side. Slipping an arm around her he asked, "What happened?" While glancing at Morgan, Frank showed his concern and pulled his wife to his side.

"I really wish you'd reconsider letting me check you out, Maggie," Morgan said.

"What's going on?" Frank asked.

Morgan had an odd look on his face as he studied Maggie. "I guess you could have picked a better time to tell him...."

Frank paled.

Maggie actually blushed. "Oh dear." Turning, she faced Frank, taking his hands in hers.

"Honey...what...?"

"I'm okay. Honestly." Glancing around at the crowd she smiled. "I wasn't sure, it's been so long and we didn't think we could so I asked Dr. Talbot not to say anything until we were certain but..."

She hesitated. Her husband squeezed her hands. Maggie turned back to her husband Frank, the local bookstore owner and smiled.

"We're going to have a little one reading books from our shelves in a few years."

Rachel gasped excitedly, knowing that Maggie had been trying forever to get pregnant.

Others did as well.

Frank only blinked. Then he blinked again. "Huh?"

The crowd chuckled.

"I'm pregnant, Frank!"

His reaction was priceless. Rachel watched his eyes bug out, his hands go toward her shoulders, pause, go down toward her hands, back toward her face then grab her hips. "Whoo-eee!"

Maggie laughed and caught her husband's shoulders and then held on as Frank whirled her around.

When he lowered her it was to catch her lips in a kiss. A very intimate and yet tender kiss. People chuckled, whistled, slapped each other on the back while waiting…and waiting…and waiting…

"Ahem," Ben finally said. "I think there are a few people who would like to say congratulations Frank."

The entire crowd laughed.

The air filled with festivities as Maggie pulled back blushing.

People surged forward.

A touch to her elbow brought Rachel's gaze around.

"Are you all right?" Morgan asked.

She nodded. "Fine. I can't believe she was playing softball. Why hadn't she told her husband?"

Morgan sighed. "Fear, probably. I had suspected she hadn't told her husband. Stepping in and saying something about her playing softball wasn't my place. After all, there's no real reason for her not to, but I was surprised Frank had let her—if he'd known. I should have asked her sooner," he added ruefully.

"Since the game seems to be over," Rachel said, deciding to change the subject, "I'll tell you something."

"What's that?" Morgan asked smiling.

"I planned to run headfirst right into you," Rachel said cheekily.

"You what?" Morgan gaped at her before his rich chuckle floated over the field.

"Revenge," she said succinctly, "for suckering me into this simple little game of ball and then telling the pitcher to cream me."

"All in fun," he murmured, reaching behind her to dust her off, then edging her toward the sidelines.

"Hey!" she protested as his hand beat the dust from her. "And mine would have been in fun, too," she muttered and went along with him.

Lindsay saw her mom coming, broke off from the women who were keeping an eye on the children and came running toward her.

Rachel caught her in her arms.

"Hi, sweetie," she said against Lindsay's cheek.

"Mo, ohn," she said, and reached for him.

Morgan caught her in midair as usual. Hugging her close, he said, "This girl is going to be a ranger one day."

"Ranger?"

"U.S. Army. Arruuugha," he murmured. "Learned about it at school."

"I take it rangers take chances?"

Morgan chuckled. "She scares me the way she does it. Children just don't have any fear, do they?"

"She loves taking chances."

"And does her mama?" Morgan asked softly, bouncing Lindsay once above his head before setting her on her feet and letting her run over to play.

"That depends. Is it safe?"

"Very safe," he murmured.

"Okay," she replied, her gaze burning into him. Morgan knew this for what it was. It was a step of faith on her part that she would allow him to do what he planned and trust him not to hurt her.

"Betty," he called to the woman walking up to the nearby group.

Betty turned and strolled over. "Yes, Morgan?"

Morgan never broke eye contact with Rachel as he said, "Watch Lindsay, please, for an hour. I'd like to take Rachel someplace special."

"Well, of course. You two go and have fun."

He knew Betty turned and walked to Lindsay. Still, he stared at Rachel. "Are you game? I promise you, it's safe."

Slowly she nodded.

Morgan moved forward and slipped a hand to her back, then quietly escorted her across the lawn to his car. He opened the door and allowed her to slide in, then closed it after her.

He dropped into his own seat and started the car.

"Are we dressed okay?" she asked.

He nodded. "You're dressed perfectly," he replied.

He pulled the car out, turned and headed down the street. "We're leaving town?" she asked.

"Not far," he replied. "I wanted to show you something. Promise."

He knew she was nervous and he couldn't blame her. After all, how much did she really know about him?

He went three miles and turned onto an unpaved overgrown road. "Your mother wondered what I did with my spare time. I wanted to show you." He pulled into an open field and stopped the car.

"This?" she asked, looking around. Bewilderment shone in her eyes as she tried to pick out just what it was he wanted her to see.

Tenderness ran through him as he watched her search. "Don't look so closely, Rachel. Look at the whole picture and tell me what you see."

Cutting her glance quickly at him she studied him, then nodded. "I see a place where a house used to stand. All that's left is a foundation. It's hard to see because the grass is so high. Brown grass. In the distance there are trees." Looking behind her, she added, "So many trees surround the area that you can't see the road from here."

Morgan nodded. "Want to know what I see, Rachel?"

Softly, her voice running over him like a soft spring rain on a warm day, she replied, "What do you see Morgan?"

"I see children. Playing, enjoying themselves as they chase each other and play tag. I see a two-story white house, with one of those old-fashioned wraparound porches. Nearby is a swing set and past that are some stables. In the trees over there is an empty bird nest waiting for its maker to return and fill it again for spring. Flowers grow around the house. And outside that house hangs a sign."

"What does the sign say?" she asked.

Morgan hesitated, then decided to trust his instinct. "Halley House."

The shifting of her body was the only sound in the quiet car. Then her hand touched his forearm. "She must have been very special."

Morgan thought of his young daughter.

"She was. Very special. Unfortunately, I realized it too late."

She shifted again, then removed her hand. He missed the warmth of her touch, of another human.

"It's never too late," Rachel said, her voice more distant than it had been a moment ago.

Morgan didn't understand at first, steeped in his memories. "She passed away," he replied, then realized what she thought. "Oh, Rachel," he whispered, turning so he could meet her gaze. "It's not a woman. Halley was my daughter."

Chapter Fourteen

"I had no idea Morgan had a daughter," Betty said, rinsing potatoes in the sink. "He never mentioned her."

"From what he said, I got the impression it was too painful for him to talk about. He did mention he wanted to build a house, have children and name the house after his child."

"He must really miss her."

"Yeah, Mom. Then, before I could ask any questions, a hawk flew over and he was out of the car and we were looking for bird nests."

"Sounds like you had a good time, dear," Betty said and moved to the table to cut the potatoes up.

Rachel wiped a cabinet. "I did." She paused before adding, "Why didn't you tell me Dr. Talbot was a specialist in pediatric audiology?"

"I figured you'd find out soon enough."

"He told me when he was talking to me about making an appointment for Lindsay for further testing."

Betty turned and studied her daughter. "How do you feel about that?"

Rachel tossed the cloth down and ran a hand through her hair. "How do you think I feel?" she said, and she knew she sounded short. "I'm sorry, Mom. I didn't mean to yell—"

Betty went to her, took her hand and pulled her to the table, and sat down. "It's all right."

Concern twisted Betty's features into such a familiar expression. How many years had she seen that expression and felt her mother was interfering? Rachel knew better now. It was a mother's love, a caring and concern she saw, not interference.

"It's going to be okay, honey," her mom said softly.

Rachel didn't release her mom's hand. "I'm so scared. I don't want another doctor telling me she needs to be put in a home or that nothing can be done."

"Morgan would never suggest you put Lindsay in a home."

"I know, but..." Rachel sighed. "I know the schools aren't supposed to be bad, and they have some wonderful things—"

"Honey, this isn't about that at all, is it?"

Startled, Rachel glanced at her.

"You're allowing Morgan to examine her. That's something you haven't allowed with any other doctor."

"Yes."

"You trust him, at least as far as that goes."

Rachel shrugged, and her gaze slid to her hands, which she noted were clasped together, an obvious sign of tension.

"You're afraid you're going to see Lindsay rejected again, just like Jim did."

Rachel flinched at her ex-husband's name. "He's just a doctor, Mom. It doesn't matter—"

"He's more than just a doctor, isn't he?"

Fear crept into Rachel. That was one thing she wanted to avoid thinking about.

"Did you see how gentle he was with Maggie when she announced her news?"

Betty nodded. "He's a good man, a caring man. Not all men are like your husband—self-centered and unwilling to try to make a marriage work."

"Is he Maggie's doctor?" Rachel asked, to change the subject. She had no desire to discuss Morgan and her husband in the same conversation. It made her mind drift to more permanent things, things she definitely shouldn't be thinking about, things that just weren't meant for her.

Betty stood and went back to working on the potatoes. "I'm not sure. I really think Maggie is too old for a pediatrician. Heaven knows, she is going to need a good doctor. I heard her brother is moving back to town."

"Brother?"

"Luke. You know how rumors are. And you know how Emma hears them all." Betty chuckled.

"You really enjoy your job at church, don't you?"

That was something Rachel still couldn't quite grasp. Betty had always been a work-at-home mom who fixed cookies, kept an immaculate house and doted on the children. She'd never dreamed her mother would want anything new. But there was a sparkle in her eyes each time she mentioned work.

"Yes, honey, I do. I know it shocks you that your mom enjoys working outside the house, doesn't it?"

"A bit."

Betty smiled at her before slipping the potatoes into the oven. "I loved taking care of your dad and you kids, Rachel. But this has opened up an entire new world. It's been wonderful to experience new things."

"Like Mr. Sinclair?"

Her mother blushed. "Warren is simply working on the day care. He had some questions and I was answering them."

"You know, Mom, it seems weird seeing you with another man, but if you, well, if you decided to…date him, or whatever you'd call it, I would approve."

Her mom's shoulders eased, and Rachel realized her mother had been worried about her reaction.

"Thank you." She sat down. "Not that I ever thought I'd be discussing this with my daughter, much less that it would happen…" Betty took Rachel's hands. "I loved your father more than life itself. But he's gone. I miss him, honey, and always will, but sometimes you just have to get on with life.''

Rachel shifted, hearing the double meaning and realizing her mom hadn't forgotten at all about Jim or their discussion of Morgan. ''Yes, eventually.''

''That's right. And Warren is a nice man. I enjoy talking with him. We're friends. We have a lot in common. I don't know if it'll go further. I'm a grandmother, for pity's sake. But then, he's old enough for that, too. Anyway, sometimes you just have to realize that there's more in life and reach out and grab it.''

Rachel dropped her gaze. ''And hope it's not fool's gold instead,'' she whispered, and wondered if she even knew the difference.

Chapter Fifteen

"She'll be fine. Don't worry."

Morgan stared at the little girl in his arms and smiled at her. "Right, Lindsay?" he signed, then smiled.

Lindsay hugged him.

"I just—" Rachel started and then broke off.

Morgan slipped an arm around her. "I think Mama needs this more than Lindsay at the moment."

"I'm sorry, Morgan. I just— I'm scared."

Rachel's petite body leaned into him, provoking feelings of comfort in Morgan. She was so small and had been through so much with her daughter. He ached for her, wished he could heal the hurt and distrust within her.

But, though he was a healer of the body, he couldn't heal souls. He had to leave Rachel in God's hands and trust Him to do the healing she required.

She stepped back.

So did he. "We're going to start with the simple hearing tests and then we'll go on to the more advanced tests. If you'd like to watch, there's a viewing room. I promise you, honey, we aren't going to hurt Lindsay."

"I know. Yes, I'd like to watch."

"Ah, well, it looks like you might not be alone." He motioned, and Rachel turned.

"Mom? Reverend Ben?"

Morgan watched as her mother smiled. Such a sweet, loving smile. Betty loved her daughter very much. "I just thought, dear, you should have someone here with you. I was talking to Ben about it, and he decided to come along."

"Oh, well, I...thank you, Reve—"

"Just Ben."

"Thank you, Ben."

Morgan interrupted them. "My nurse will show you where to go. Lindsay and I are going before she gets impatient." He grinned at the little girl. "Make yourselves at home. These tests are going to take anywhere from an hour to an hour and a half."

Rachel knew that. She remembered him explaining to her that Lindsay would have several breaks during the time so she wouldn't get too tired. She watched her baby being taken off by a doctor once again and wondered how that had happened.

"It'll be okay, honey," Betty said, coming up next to her.

Reminding herself this was Morgan, Morgan who had shown his desire to be Lindsay's friend, Morgan who took Lindsay fishing, Morgan who had kissed her...

"I know," she said, shaking off that last image. "I know it will."

"Shall we go, ladies?" Ben asked as the nurse waved them after her down the hall.

Rachel quietly followed the nurse, who was dressed in blue and white teddy bear scrubs, down the sterile white halls. The hollow sound of their feet echoing on the tiled floor was the only noise besides the PA system, paging doctors in the background.

They turned at a side hall and the nurse stopped. "In here. There's coffee and tea and they usually have muffins. Colas and other foods are in the vending machines near the cafeteria.''

''We'll be fine, thanks,'' Ben said, and Rachel didn't object as he led them into the room.

The room was dark, lit only by two small lamps that sat on end tables. There was an emerald sofa with four matching overstuffed chairs, and sure enough, against the wall were a tiny sink, a coffeepot and disposable coffee cups.

''Oh, my, look at that room, Rachel.''

''Yeah, Mom,'' Rachel said, moving toward the chair positioned nearest the wall. Wrapping her arms around herself, she sank onto the edge of the chair.

The room was certainly set up to entertain children. Rachel had expected a room as sterile as the halls outside. But this room wasn't like that at all. The walls were painted with bright, primary colors depicting scenes of a forest teeming with life. She saw rabbits, deer and birds, all painted in bright colors.

The carpet was wall to wall and had tiny little roads drawn on it. She noted other pieces of different colored carpet in different areas and realized that each section was a testing section.

"Ah, there they are now," Ben said quietly, and pulled a chair from the tiny table in the corner next to Rachel.

She didn't say it, but in some odd way, that simple gesture meant so much to her. "She's okay."

Ben chuckled. "More than okay, I'd say. She looks downright happy."

Rachel relaxed an indefinable amount. "Maybe. But they haven't started the testing yet."

Her mother pulled out a book. "She's going to be just fine. Just relax, sweetheart."

She wondered if her mom really believed that she still fell for that read-a-book-and-look-nonchalant routine. Rachel had learned a long time ago, when her mom brought a book with her somewhere, it was because she was worried.

"Of course she will," Rachel murmured and returned her attention to the room.

"Was your daughter deaf at birth, Rachel?" Ben asked.

From a distance Rachel watched her daughter throw her hands up and take off at a dead run toward a slide. "I'm not sure. We, um, Jim and I, we didn't notice at first. She was a loud baby. Cried a lot. It bothered Jim."

Morgan slipped off his shoes, dropped onto the floor and started playing with her.

"Some babies certainly can kick up a fuss. I'd say as active as she is, she must have been an active baby."

"Not a lot," Rachel said absently as she watched Lindsay slide down and then toss a ball with Morgan. "Jim didn't like noise."

Morgan played, then led her to a table. They sat down and he put earphones on both of them and opened books. He was signing something to her as he talked, but Rachel couldn't read what. He lifted his hand and then flipped a page.

Then he nodded to his nurse, who was across the room, and she realized they were testing and Lindsay had no idea what they were up to. Rachel relaxed a bit more.

"When did you finally figure out she had trouble hearing?"

"Hmm? Oh, well, about a year ago. Her speech wasn't developing like the other children her age, and she ignored us quite a bit. Jim thought she was being stubborn but...but she's such a happy child. The dichotomy in her just didn't set right. I took her to a few doctors before that, but this one I took her to, this one said that…''

When she didn't finish, Ben changed the subject. ''Spring practice for basketball starts up soon. I'm planning to coerce that doctor in there into helping me.''

Rachel looked around, surprised. ''He plays basketball?''

''Not yet,'' Ben said, grinning.

Rachel laughed.

Ben returned her smile. ''He said he used to play it as a kid. I plan to draft him into it.''

''I don't suppose that's something you forget.''

''No. And I just got a new hoop put up. I have to constantly thank God for Morgan.''

Surprised, Rachel turned again to look at Ben. ''You have children?''

Ben shook his head and crossed an ankle over his right knee as he leaned back. ''No. But I'm new here and meeting with just a tad bit of resistance.''

Betty's snort told Rachel she heard more than she let on.

''Okay, there are many who think I'm too

young to be in charge of the church. Anyway," he said, tossing a stop-that look at Betty, who had snorted again, "Morgan has been a strong steady friend to me. There are days that his friendship really helped me through problems. He's a good, godly man. Doesn't stick his nose in where it's not wanted—most of the time," he added, grinning at her.

"He's not interfering," Rachel said softly, and the last of her worry fled. "He and Lindsay have developed a special bond."

"I see that." Ben nodded toward the glass.

Rachel turned just in time to see Lindsay give Morgan a kiss. A smile touched Rachel's lips, and tears came to her eyes. "Why couldn't Jim have been like that? Why did he give up so easily?"

"I think he gave up a long time before your child was born, didn't he, Rachel?"

Dropping her gaze to her hands, she whispered, "Yes. But how can anyone not love a child?"

A strong, gentle hand squeezed her shoulder. "I wish I had an answer for that one, Rachel. I really do."

No more words were exchanged as they

watched Lindsay for the next half hour. Then Morgan and Lindsay disappeared into another room. They were gone nearly thirty minutes before Morgan returned with a sleeping Lindsay in his arms.

"Well?" Rachel asked nervously, standing when she saw Morgan walk in. Betty beat her to Morgan and took the sleeping child from him. Rachel paused to run a hand over her hair before turning to Morgan. It didn't bother her in the least when Ben walked over and stroked Lindsay's cheek and said a soft, quick little prayer of healing and comfort. Her attention was focused on Morgan, with what she had hoped never to face again—hope. Hope brought fear. Fear of rejection, of no answer, of suggestions for treatment she didn't want to think about.

"There is some nerve damage, it looks like, Rachel. But then, you pretty much had already been told that. I'll have the test results in a few days and can tell you more."

Morgan must have sensed Rachel's anxiety because he pulled her into his arms and hugged her. "The good news is there is probably a treatment."

"I don't want her going through any painful treatments or…or anything like that."

"You have all the time in the world, Rachel, to decide what you want. Why don't we go get some lunch? It's almost lunchtime."

"Oh!" Rachel glanced at her watch, then at her mom and Ben. "I guess I hadn't realized it'd been that long. Then again, it seems like it was much longer."

"I can't," Betty said apologetically. "I need to get back to work, and I think Lindsay here will be ready for nap time."

"Ben?" Morgan asked.

"I should get back, too. I'm meeting with Jason later. He wanted to come by and talk. He's a good kid."

Rachel recognized that name. She remembered an older couple at church who were giving Ben a rather long lecture. Rachel wondered if those were his parents and if the child was anything like them.

"Well, Rachel. Are you going to desert me, too?" Morgan asked, and gave her such a sorrowful look she couldn't help but laugh.

"I have the entire day off because of these tests. I'm sure I can spare an hour for lunch."

"Great," Morgan said, his boyish look pulling another grin from her.

"Oh." She turned to face Ben. "Thank you, Ben, for coming over. Your support meant a lot to me."

He gave her a gentle smile and nodded. "Anytime, Rachel. That's what we're here for."

He turned and ambled down the hall.

"Honey, why don't you take the rest of the day off and let me keep Lindsay? She won't mind staying in day care or with me an extra hour or so."

Rachel hesitated. The offer was tempting. Finally, she nodded. "Very well."

"Give Lindsay a kiss so I can go," Betty commanded.

Rachel did just that, hurrying forward and leaning close. Pushing her daughter's curls out of the way, Rachel kissed her on the forehead.

Lindsay sighed and turned her head, snuggling against Betty.

Rachel's heart filled with love as she watched. Looking at her mom, she said softly, "Thanks, Mom."

"Any time." She walked briskly down the

hall to where Ben waited. Together, the two turned the corner and disappeared from sight.

Then she was alone with Morgan.

The air seemed suddenly charged as they stood there, the occasional echo of a voice, the speakers, elevators, all flowing together into a cacophony of music that every hospital she'd ever been in sang to its visitors and patients.

"Well."

"Having second thoughts, Rachel?"

Slowly she shook her head. "No, Morgan. Actually, for the first time, I'm having no second thoughts at all."

It was in that instant she realized she'd fallen for Morgan, and fallen hard. She stared at him, trying to absorb the shock of her sudden knowledge.

"You may," he murmured, and reached to take her hand.

"What—?" she asked, trying to drag her thoughts into some semblance of order.

With a grin, he replied, "I confess. I knew you had the whole day off and arranged for a friend to take my appointments for the afternoon. By the time I return you home this evening, you may wish you had never met me."

Uh-oh. "Morgan?" she asked, uneasiness

creeping into her. "What are we doing? What are you up to?"

With a grin, he slipped an arm around her and guided her toward an exit door. "We're going for a jousting."

So stunned was Rachel, she didn't say another word the entire way to the car.

Chapter Sixteen

"I don't believe it. A castle? Here? I mean, I'd heard there was a place like this, but seriously, I had no idea—it's shaped like a castle!"

Morgan grinned from ear to ear. He couldn't help it. The look on Rachel's face was priceless. "A castle for the lady," he murmured, and pushed open his door.

And indeed it was a castle, gray stone, banners flying from the parapets, the entire look. It was a façade, of course, but still, it did look awfully realistic. "They have a medieval festival here every spring. It's not well publicized. But it's certainly interesting to attend."

He watched her gaze go over the people coming and going, some with children, others in groups and couples. She finally turned to him and grinned. "This looks wonderful."

"I'm glad you think so." He slipped a hand to her back and led her to the door, where he paid.

"This way, ma'am," the young woman at the gate said after checking her hand for the stamp.

"Um, wait, I—" She looked at Morgan.

With a sly grin, he said, "Did I forget to mention certain packages allow costumes?"

"Yes, you did." She returned his grin.

"I'll meet you out front."

She gave him a soft smile and hurried off. He went with the young man into another room and specified what he wanted. Of course, they were out of the medieval outfits, so he moved up in years.

If Rachel had any idea how much he'd paid she would hit the roof. With a grin, he thought it was worth it just to see her expression.

The young man brought a costume, and he accepted it. "I hate these things," Morgan muttered to the boy as he pulled on teal tights.

"Most do who come in here," he replied.

"That's why the medieval outfits go first. Less colorful, more cloth."

"I'm Morgan, by the way."

"Pete. I work here spring break and summertime."

"You enjoy your work?" Morgan donned a teal undertunic with lace at the end of the sleeves before pulling on the darker green and gold jacket. He picked up the floppy beret with a feather and plopped it on his head. "I actually prefer the medieval costumes. A shame you're out of those," he muttered.

"Yeah, it can be fun. I'm training to be an assistant to one of the groups here. I hope to work full-time this summer in one of the skits."

"Good luck." With a tug at the outrageous green vest and a straightening of the other bits and pieces that made up his costume, Morgan donned his shoes and left.

Inside the main entrance, he stopped, entranced. Rachel stood there, dressed from head to toe in red and gold. Her dress had a square-cut neck with a high waist, and the fabric fell in waves around her. The sleeves were a bit too short, as was the skirt, but no one would notice. Tiny gold butterflies decorated the material. The crown, though, was what caught and held his attention. A sheer piece of ruby red fabric caught up with a circlet of faux pearls was worked into her hair, which had been pinned up. It fell softly over her shoulders. The color against her cheeks made her glow.

Until she saw him.

Her eyes widened.

He cocked a hip, pointed his toe and flipped off his hat before elaborately bowing.

She burst into laughter. "Jade!" she said, attempting to control her laughter but gaining little control.

"I'll have you know this is teal. It says so on the tag."

"Oh, of course. Forgive me. Teal. Much better."

He lifted a shin, turning it first one way and then the next. "I happen to think I look mighty fine in teal."

"Okay, okay, you look so fine in it, I'm sure the day you marry you'll end up wearing teal. It's just so nice on you."

She giggled again.

Morgan's gaze shot to hers. "I just might," he murmured, and smiled, wondering if she would like to see him in a teal cummerbund. Her smile faded.

He backed off, seeing the glimmer of desire in her eyes. "Shall we go?" He motioned her on.

With a nod, she started down the wide dirt path. Stores lined the street, and renaissance music played. In the distance he heard a dulcimer and King Henry and his wife wandered past.

"Where are we going?" Rachel asked.

"Where do you want to go?"

"Well, I hate to say it, but I am a bit hungry."

He checked his watch. "They start a new meal in twenty minutes. We can go to that one if you want."

"Start a new meal? I don't understand." She turned to him, and a loose strand of hair blew into her face.

He brushed it away. "Yes. They serve meals at trestle tables. Not individual seatings. So every three hours they have a meal."

"Three hours!"

Resting his hand on the hilt of the plastic sword strapped to his side, he nodded. "They have entertainment, as well. You want to eat now or wait until the next seating, which will actually be their first suppertime serving? They have torches then in their procession. Afternoon meals only have banners.''

"I take it you've come here before."

"Three or four times," he murmured.

Looking around her, Rachel tried to decide what to do. There was so much to see, but then, she was hungry, too. She hadn't had breakfast, too worried about Lindsay.

"Let's eat."

"Your wish," he murmured and lifted her hand and kissed it—again.

Rachel shivered, thinking she could really get used to that. Such a simple act made her feel so ridiculously feminine. She liked that.

He placed his hand on her back. "This way."

He guided her across the street and down the wooden sidewalk until they came to their destination. She knew they were there long before they reached it. She could tell by all the people standing around in groups waiting.

Some wore regular street clothes. A few of the brave ones were in shorts. But many were dressed in a rainbow of bright, cheery colors and soft flowing pastels. She saw everything from chain mail to skirts to musketeer outfits. One woman was dressed as a musketeer, but most women wore dresses like the one she wore, or garments of later styles. Some wore frilly little things around their necks. She had no idea what they were.

"Is that chain mail real?" she whispered as one man covered in tiny gray rings with a big white tunic over them strode toward a group near the back of the crowd.

"I doubt it. Real chain mail is very heavy, very very expensive and wouldn't be comfortable to wear around. Look at what your dress is made of. Cool breathing material. So is mine. Cheap, nice looking, tending to give the look of the era, but unreal."

"How do you know all of this? It's not required reading for doctors."

"I had time after I graduated from medical school. I wanted to fill my evening hours with something. So, I did reading hour at the library and spent a lot of time there simply researching on my off time. The kids loved reading time. They loved stories of knights and damsels and—"

"And that's where you picked up the way to treat kids like that!"

"Yeah."

Rachel heard the affirmation but saw something in his eyes, something that looked like regret. She started to answer him when two loud trumpets sounded.

She nearly landed on Morgan's shoe after jumping two feet in the air. Grabbing her heart, she looked at him. "You could have warned me."

"Think medieval," he said, chuckling.

"I have never read anything medieval. The most I know is, um, Robin Hood."

"You're in for a treat, then."

"If you say so."

Chapter Seventeen

Rachel was enchanted. Not.

Looking around, she saw a tiered arena surrounded by a fence with tables all around. In the middle was a ring filled with dirt and hay. Things that reminded her of sawhorses were in the ring.

"What in the world?"

Morgan chuckled and slid his hand to her back. "Come this way. You'll see."

Men in uniforms and armor walked among the crowd, shouting out threats and insults at each other. It didn't take long for Rachel to figure it out. "They're part of the entertainment, aren't they?"

"Yes. Note each one has the same type of uniform and armor. However, one is wearing blue, one red, one white and one green."

"Opposing armies?" Glancing at him in question, she allowed herself to be guided to a table near the front row. There weren't too many people here, which made it nice.

"My lady, allow me!" Rachel turned, surprised, as a man in the red armor came up to her.

She looked at Morgan, who stared at the knight.

"I, um," she began, not sure what to say.

Going down on one knee, he said, "You wear my colors, and it would do me great honor to receive a favor from you for I am to ride into battle against the Scourge of Harlan soon."

"A favor?"

"He's wanting something to wear on his armor."

The knight grinned cheekily at Morgan. "'Tis true, my lord, that I seek favor from your beloved."

Rachel felt her cheeks heating up. As the man opened his mouth to continue, she tore off the filmy headdress. "Here! Take this," she commanded. Anything to get rid of him, she thought, certain she was the color of her dress by now.

"Ah, a favor!" He stood and waved it at the crowd, who cheered.

"Oh, no, they are watching us," she moaned.

Morgan chuckled. "Do my lady justice on the field, Sir Knight," Morgan murmured. "Or I'll have to find you and make you pay for the embarrassment you have caused her."

The actor playing the knight threw back his head and laughed before clapping Morgan on the shoulder and walking off. He promptly strutted over to the man in green and waved the favor in his face.

"Oh, dear," Rachel whispered. "This is so embarrassing."

"Here. Sit. It won't be so bad now."

She sat. "Why did he pick me?" Rachel asked, smiling weakly at the others who sat with them at the table. They all smiled back and wished her luck.

"As he said, my lady, it was the colors you wear."

Morgan leaned close after saying that. Rachel leaned toward him for some privacy. The warmth from his breath caressed her cheek as he said, "It could be the dress, but I think it be far more likely 'tis the bloom in my lady's cheek, the gentle wash of color that caresses the..."

"Morgan!" she whispered, her cheeks going up in flames.

He chuckled. "Okay, okay. I'll allow you peace during lunch."

"Thank you," she murmured, though a small smile escaped her. "My cheeks, hmm?"

"Ah, here's the food," he replied.

Rachel's eyes widened as she watched the huge plates of food being brought out and set before each person. "Are we supposed to eat all of this?" she asked, shoving her hair behind her ear.

On her plate was carved meat and vegetables, a huge piece of bread and a small round something in the middle. Sauce, cranberries maybe.

"Not at all. Ah, look, the entertainment is about to begin."

Rachel glanced up. Sure enough a procession of musicians was just entering the ring. "I can't believe this. Does this go on all the time? I'd love to bring Lindsay here some-time.''

"I bet she'd love it. I only wish..."

"What?" she asked softly, turning to him. She could see the regret in his eyes, a look of despair. A burst of laughter from those around them distracted her, and the moment was passed. Morgan lifted his fork and took a bite of meat.

"Where are you from, Morgan?" she asked, and began to eat as the entertainers sang, danced and juggled.

"The big city. I grew up there."

Surprised, she nodded. "I worked there for years until returning here a few weeks ago. Why did you leave?"

He swallowed and took a sip of tea from his goblet. "I realized there were some things more important than the rat race. I wanted somewhere to..."

When he paused, she asked, "Recoup? Recover? Isn't that why everyone leaves a practice or a possibility for a good practice. After all, with your specialty you could be making five times what you're making here."

Morgan cut another piece of meat and stabbed it. "I could be, yes. I suppose, though,

God had to get me out here to teach me that there are many, many things more important than money and a career.''

"How long have you been a doctor, Morgan?'' She knew she was being nosy, but just listening to his deep rumbling voice was so nice.

"Less than five years, actually.''

"Really?''

"Yeah, well, medical school takes a bit longer than four years.''

"That's why I'm an accountant.''

He chuckled. "Oh? How does medical school and being an accountant relate?''

She grinned before taking a bite, chewing and swallowing. She finally said, "One you spend your life in college, the other you only have to give up four years of your life.''

He did laugh then, deep, rumbling, the lines on his face easing and making him look younger than his years. "You disliked school that much?'' he asked.

"No. I wanted to have children that badly.''

He sobered. "And you did,'' he said softly.

"Not at first. I had my entire life planned out. I would go to school and then work for a year or so before meeting Mr. Right and marrying. Then we'd be married for a year and then have children.''

"But?" he asked, encouraging her.

Smiling, she pushed the last of her food away. "It didn't work that way. I got my degree and fell in love with one of the people who was there on a job search. He was scoping out possible people to work for him."

"Jim?" he asked, and Rachel nodded, thinking Morgan probably knew what was coming. It was so typical.

"Yes. He saw me, wined me and dined me. I got a job but within six months we were married. Soon after he suggested I stay home to help him with the parties he'd need to throw. At first, I thought it sounded okay. But I was bored quickly. That's when I found out he had no intention of letting me work at the company. He said he had a policy against family working there. The policy was really his secretary, though I didn't know it yet. I was disappointed, but then I found out I was pregnant.''

Rachel saw knights coming out on the field. "Look." She pointed.

Morgan's hand touched hers and squeezed.

She didn't ask him to remove it but curved her own around his. "I'm sorry," Morgan said.

"Don't be. When Jim found out I was pregnant he hit the roof. He was furious because he didn't want children. They'd interfere with my ability to take care of him."

"Stingy, wasn't he?" Morgan murmured. He released her hand, and she heard him move his chair. Then he was next to her seated and taking her hand between his two warm ones.

"I guess I was, too. He wanted me to have an abortion, but I refused. Nor would I give the baby up for adoption. But this was my baby. My marriage was a farce and I thought, with this child, maybe things would get better, at least I'd have someone to love."

"What about God, Rachel?"

Rachel shook her head. "I—well, Jim didn't go to church. Oh, he did at first, but after we were married... Anyway, I have decided that possibly God just doesn't care for us on a day-to-day basis. Why would He allow my child to be born like this, the ultimate thing that broke up our marriage? Why would he allow Lindsay to be fatherless?" she whispered.

"The bible says that God's ways aren't always our ways, Rachel. Perhaps He wants everything to turn out even better for you and Lindsay.''

Rachel squeezed his hand, hoping that was true but just unable to believe. What would it take for her to simply believe again?

Faith. Simple faith.

Maybe, God, you might care. Maybe, but I'm just not sure. Help me to believe.

''Oh, look. The red knight just defeated his opponent.''

Rachel looked, and sure enough, the other man was on the ground. The red knight walked his horse around the ring, grinning, until he got to where she and Morgan sat. Then the knight stopped. He turned and raised a hand. ''My lady's favor brought me success this day.''

A young girl walked out with a floral wreath that had ribbons and bells hanging down, decorated in reds and blues and pinks and purples. She handed it to the knight. ''Fair lady, this is for you, crowned the fairest at the ceremony today.'' He held it out, acting like the dancing of the horse as he leaned sideways wasn't affecting him in the least.

Before she could rise and get it, Morgan stood and lifted a brow. ''I'll place it on my lady's head.''

The red knight laughed loud. "Keep this one, my lady. He's a good man."

He mounted and then signaled his horse, which jumped to obey its master and they raced off together toward the exit.

Rachel groaned. "I don't believe it."

She smiled as Morgan slipped the floral wreath upon her head.

"Embarrassed again?"

"I'm beginning to think I would not have made a very good lady if I had to listen to people like him all the time."

Morgan chuckled. Music started up. He reached for her hand and urged her to stand. "Come with me," he murmured.

His eyes bade her, and she followed, glad to be off the subject of her past, of his past, and back in the now, with him looking at her with such tenderness and such ardor. What was it about him? Why did he seem to have such a hold on her life? It was only a few weeks ago she met him, but for some reason, she felt as if she'd known him her entire life.

"Wait a minute." Looking around, she realized he led her onto the grounds where they had just watched the jousting. "What are we doing out here?"

He grinned that boyish grin that melted her right down to her toes. "We're going to dance."

"But...but I can't dance."

"This is easy. It's an old medieval dance the host is calling us to. It won't take you any time at all to pick up the steps."

He was right. It didn't. In just a few short minutes, she was moving with him and about a dozen others in a way she had only seen on TV. It was new, it was fun, but most of all, it was so romantic that Rachel wished the dance would never end.

Holding hands and curtsying, then walking and turning and twirling as, one by one, the line moved, Rachel found she still didn't lose sight of Morgan across from her. His gaze was on her, warm and tender, and she couldn't help but return it.

She had come to Fairweather expecting heartache and loneliness as she attempted to eke out a living. Instead, she'd tumbled with a bang right into Morgan Talbot's arms.

The music had them turning. Then she and Morgan came face to face. She remembered the feel of him that day, much like now, as he held her hands and they made their way down the line. This was so much more, though. This wasn't just a good-looking stranger that she'd run into but a handsome, caring man who had captured her mother's nurturing spirit, her daughter's endless joy and her...

The music ended. Morgan pulled her forward. "You're beautiful when you dance, Rachel," he murmured and then slipped his arms around her, lowered his head and kissed her.

She felt joy surge through her to every end of every hair on her head. She wouldn't be surprised if her hair was standing straight up, the kiss affected her so.

But not just the kiss. Because Rachel had just realized something much more important than a kiss.

With amazement, Rachel knew that Morgan had captured her heart.

Chapter Eighteen

Morgan stared at the lovely woman in his arms. It was time to come clean, he thought. He had to tell her about everything in his past so she would know. Then he would talk to her, tell her his feelings.

"I love you," Rachel said.

Morgan stared at her lips, certain he hadn't heard what she'd just said.

"I love you." Nor had he repeated those words to her. The look in her eyes confirmed that he had indeed repeated the words. And with those words, they both had complicated this relationship more than Rachel knew. Still, he couldn't stop himself. He leaned down and kissed her again.

She responded, tilting her head and, after a small hesitation, squeezing him tight.

Pulling back, he took her hands. Oh, boy, this is getting out of control quick. Morgan felt like he'd just been hit by a snowball that seemed small but was actually the size of a Mack truck. He had to talk to her—now.

The glow on her face made him hesitate.

Father, what am I going to do now? he silently asked. I have to tell her.

But later.

He'd wait until they left. He couldn't tell her now. How would that look?

It would look like he'd been waiting for her to fall in love with him before he confessed his deep, dark secret.

He would have to wait. There was no other way to do it.

Together they left the dining hall and made their rounds to visit the apothecary, a costume shop, a souvenir shop and displays. They watched two sword fights, a hawking demonstration, and they ate again before it grew dark.

And during the entire time, Rachel never again spoke those three words she'd said to him earlier. But he knew she meant them. Her looks had turned shy, nervous. She radiated a cautious joy in her gaze. She hadn't meant to blurt them out, he could tell that. But now that she had and he had returned them, there was a careful trust in her actions as she took his hand when they walked, leaned a bit more into him as they talked, inched closer when they sat.

These were little things she probably didn't realize she did, but things that told him she had finally let down her guard and accepted him within her defined space as a safe person.

He felt horrible for that misplaced trust.

He felt guilty for not talking to her before now. But the time had just never seemed to come up. Lindsay had been there, or someone else, or because of testing...

"Are you ready to go?" he asked, looking at her.

She smiled at him. "Yes. I'm tired, and Lindsay will be going to bed soon. I've had a wonderful time, though."

"So have I, sweetheart. Let me change, and I'll be right out."

He separated from her and quickly donned his street clothes before meeting her out front. Tucking her into the car, he moved around to his side and slid in. With a quiet hum, the car started, and they were on their way down the dark highway.

"I wonder if Lindsay will be in bed when I get home?"

"What time does she normally go to bed?" he asked and punched a small dial that illuminated a clock.

"Seven-thirty."

The clock showed nine.

"You think she'll wait up this late?" Morgan asked.

"I doubt it. She'll try, but she rarely makes it past eight-thirty."

"She is something," Morgan murmured. "Energetic and so full of life and love."

"Well, *I* think so. But, I *am* her mother."

He heard a soft sigh, then her hesitant words. "I don't know how she turned out so loving. Her father certainly didn't love her."

"Perhaps he just didn't know how to deal with it or hadn't learned just how important she was," Morgan said.

"He was stingy," Rachel replied, and he could hear the pain in her voice. "And now he'll never have a chance to change or to know his daughter."

"Yeah." Morgan felt a knot in his stomach at her words.

"Morgan, I have to ask, but I..."

"What, sweetheart?" Concerned, he glanced quickly at her. They hit the edge of town. A street lamp caught her face, throwing it into stark planes and curves. He thought, at that moment, he was seeing all the hurt, the pain, the emptiness she had felt battling her way through her daughter's problem and a husband's rejection.

"Do you...care for Lindsay?"

He turned down the street that led to Rachel's house. "Of course I do. Why in the world do you ask that?"

Then it hit him—like a ton of bricks. "She's very special to me, Rachel. You have no idea how much."

He turned onto her street and slowed.

"Oh, Morgan—" she began, but he cut her off.

"Please, Rachel, let me tell you just how much."

He eased the car to a stop in front of her house and put it in park before turning and focusing his attention on her.

Curiosity and hope shone in her eyes. Oh, Rachel. I'm so sorry.

He took her hands and squeezed them. They were alive with warmth as she wrapped her fingers around his.

"What is it, Morgan?"

"When I first saw your daughter, Rachel, I took a special interest in her. Not because your mother asked me to or because I thought it might provide a way for me to meet you again. I decided the day we ran into each other that God had sent you here for me. You're the woman I want to marry. But I saw you were hurting and knew it had to be in God's time.

"Then I saw your daughter. She's partially deaf. She's handicapped. She's imperfect."

Her hands tightened, and she pulled slightly, but he refused to release her. "Hear me out. That drew me to her, Rachel, opening my heart, making me all that more willing to love her."

"She's not charity, Morgan," Rachel whispered in a tiny, pained voice.

"No, she's not. Oh, Rachel." He took a deep breath and continued. "I had a daughter once, Rachel. She would be five years old now."

Rachel relaxed. "I'm sorry, Morgan." Leaning forward, she tried to slide her arms around him.

"No, baby. Listen."

Holding those hands in his, he drew strength then said, "Yes, it was horrible—one of the worst things that could have happened. She had cerebral palsy."

"I—I don't understand."

Morgan shuddered. "I was in my last year of medical school. The hours were ferocious. I had to make contacts, network, work hard to get where I wanted to be."

Tension curled her fingers in his hands. He wanted to pull her forward and hug her, weep over what he was about to say, but he couldn't. The pain was too deep. The pain he was going to cause *her* was too deep for him to take that liberty.

"What are you saying?" she whispered, her voice harsh and low in the car. Her breathing picked up slightly, going shallow.

"I told my wife we couldn't have children. I *told* her we had to wait another year or two after I got my career on firm ground. I was driven to be the best, have the best practice, and a child would have interfered with that. I didn't want her to have the child, but she got pregnant anyway.''

"You didn't want the child?" Rachel demanded, low.

"I was furious with my wife. I felt like she had tricked me, to risk my career like she did, Rachel. Or at least, that's how I saw it at the time. Our marriage fell to a shambles over the deceit and my own struggle between career and family.''

"You didn't want her," Rachel said again.

Finally, he shook his head. "No, I didn't. But then she was born. She was beautiful but imperfect. My wife blamed me for it and just left the hospital without authorization, taking the baby with her.''

Rachel cried out in pain. Her cry shot through him to the marrow of his bones. She jerked against his hold, her hands icy, the life gone from them.

"No, Morgan. Stop! I don't want to hear this."

Sobbing, she tried to pull away again.

"I had realized when I'd seen the baby that things would have to change. I was going to talk to Sarah and tell her I'd been foolish. But she didn't believe me. She didn't believe I had

changed. My career was first. I was served
with divorce papers. That's when I found out
she didn't have the child. You see, she blamed
me for an imperfect child, yet she didn't want
to have that imperfect child, either.''

"Sarah put the baby into a home." A sob
escaped Rachel, one that sounded pure pain.

"I started a search for my daughter as soon
as I realized she wasn't with my wife, but it
was too late. She had died a few weeks before,
in the home."

He released her hands.

Chest heaving, she grabbed at her seat belt,
trembling. "How could you!" she cried in anger and pain.

"I was selfish." He could say nothing else,
guilt and pain surrounding him in his miserable isolation.

"You deserted her. You left Lindsay—left
her fatherless!"

Morgan heard the mistake and realized she
was flashing back to Jim. He had become Jim
in her mind. He couldn't argue. He was Jim in
his own mind.

"I'd do anything to change things. But it's
too late, Rachel. We can't go back."

Finally managing to release her seat belt she

shoved the door open. "That's right. Don't come near my daughter. I'm not going through this again. How could you do this, Morgan? In a home! A home!"

He pushed out of his seat, opened the door. "Rachel, I'm sorry—"

"No. Stay there!" Sobbing uncontrollably, she turned toward the house. "I can walk myself in. Goodbye, Morgan."

She bolted. He could think of no other word to describe the sprint to her house. She was running. Running from her past, from her pain, from what he'd just told her.

With a weary sigh Morgan watched her run inside and close the door without looking back.

Wearily, his shoulders slumped. He'd just lost the woman he loved.

What was he going to do now?

Chapter Nineteen

"Morgan? What are you doing here so late?" Ben pulled open the door, concern creasing his brow. "What's the matter?"

Morgan could only stare at Ben, his heart breaking into pieces. Pain had driven him off from Rachel's house. Pain and despair. A numbing emptiness drove him to his pastor. Darkness surrounded him like a death shroud, pain from the past, the present, pain from losing Rachel. "Can you talk a bit, Ben?"

"Always," he said. Morgan walked in and sat down in one of the armchairs. Ben's house was simply decorated, the furniture having been supplied by the church. A sofa and two chairs, in neutral colors, a carpet that really needed to be replaced. The coffee table had magazines and a basketball cap. Ben loved basketball. No pictures of family on the walls. No pictures, he noted blankly. Empty, like he felt. White walls with no color to break the bleakness.

Ben walked quietly across the room, past the dining table and into the kitchen. Morgan heard the fridge open and close before Ben returned with a couple of sodas.

Morgan took the drink Ben offered and noted how chilled it was. "This feels like Rachel's hands," he murmured. "Cold. Wet with tears."

"What happened, brother?" Ben asked softly, using the affectionate term often used by members of the church. He dropped onto the sofa, sprawling in a relaxed manner, legs spread out before him, cola held between his hands. His eyes gave him away, though.

Morgan saw the compassion and alertness that said he was listening to every word, cataloguing every movement he made. That very alertness and willingness to listen were what finally helped Morgan tell Ben everything.

"She fell in love, and I crushed her heart."

Silence fell in the room like the aftermath of a death toll resonating into a cold, dark night. Silence, that is, until Morgan broke into tears and started sobbing. Morgan couldn't believe he had finally broken down. After years of guilt and grieving, he'd thought all the pain and emptiness locked away. Instead, it had only been slumbering, waiting for someone to trigger it and remind him, make him face what had happened. Vaguely, he felt someone move next to him and lay a hand on his back. He heard Ben's low tones. He knew Ben understood the tears weren't as much for Rachel as for Morgan's dead daughter. He had never let go, he realized. Never released all that pain. He'd kept it inside. If he had, he'd have mentioned it to Rachel before now. He cried out to God, praying for forgiveness, for restoration, for release from self-condemnation. Slowly, so very slowly, God's miracle happened. The pain and horror and guilt of what he had done slid from him, away into the sea of forgetfulness as God wrapped His loving spirit around Morgan and filled him with peace.

Gradually the tears dried and silence once again reigned in the room. This time there was no pain, but a gentle sound of renewal and peace. And into this soft spirit of serenity, Morgan found himself repeating his entire story to Ben.

"I was so caught up in my career, my own needs, Ben, that she died. It was my own selfishness and need. I would give anything if I could have saved her. And now Rachel is terrified history is going to repeat itself in me," he finished. "She's afraid that if I get too near them, I'll end up rejecting her daughter. I've never seen such panic and fear and hurt in anyone's eyes—except my wife's. Sarah looked that way just before she left me. We were both so full of bitterness and anger."

"If only we had sat down and talked before the baby was born. Looking back, I realize her deceit made me angrier than our having a child. She purposely set out to deceive me, and I walked around for most of her pregnancy with a wounded pride, thinking my job so very important."

"By the time the baby was born, she was sleeping in a different room, refusing to talk to me. I had hoped after the baby's birth, things would ease. She would accept my job instead of telling me to quit—quit! If I loved her I would quit and do something that would keep me home with her.'' Morgan sighed wearily. ''I only wanted to finish school, get my career started and then we could settle down and be a family.'' He shook his head. ''I never even told her I would accept the child. I was so wrapped up in my own world, Ben, and the problems between us, that I let a stream turn into an ocean of separation.

''She sneaked out of the hospital, disappeared from town and had me served with divorce papers.'' Looking at Ben, he whispered, ''The only thing that alerted me that Sarah didn't have the baby was the fact that I asked about custody of the child. Now Rachel...''

''Rachel isn't going anywhere. At least we know that.''

''Why are you so sure?'' Morgan asked. He and Ben talked a lot. Sometimes Ben was very sure of himself and other times he wasn't. But now, he sounded sure, firm, with complete assurance that Rachel would be there.

Ben stood, walked to the sofa and resumed his relaxed position. He took a swig of his cola then leaned back. ''Easy. This is her home. She lives here. Her daughter is in school here. And,'' he said and paused, allowing a twinkle to enter his eyes, "you said God sent her into your life forever and ever."

Morgan chuckled. It sounded a bit rusty, but at least he could chuckle. He reached for his cola and drank a portion of it before sitting back. "Yeah, I did, didn't I?"

"Did you mean it? Do you really believe God sent this woman into your life to share forever after with?"

Morgan took another sip of cola to give himself time to frame an answer. Did he really believe that? Or had it simply been Lindsay or his attraction? "Yes. I really believe He did, Ben. I can't explain it. But it was something— I just knew, in my heart, right there in the hall, that she was mine and I was hers." Glancing at Ben, he added, "She owns my heart. I can't imagine living without Rachel. Without Lindsay."

Silence fell, an easy one, as he contemplated what it would be like—and realized, indeed, he could not even imagine life without Rachel and Lindsay there with him. He had been asleep, dormant, until they had come into his life. Something changed the day Rachel ran into him. Lindsay changed him further with her abounding love and acceptance of him. He could give again, wanted to give. Not as a sacrifice, as he had been doing for years, not out of duty, but out of love, out of the abundance of his heart.

Ben broke the silence. "God keeps His promises, brother. Are you going to believe that all of this will work together for what is best and for what you know God has promised you in your heart?"

Morgan listened to the quiet but strong words Ben offered him. Inside, a spark of renewal ignited and slowly flickered to life. "I hurt her," he said. "She was devastated."

"And you'll hurt her again. And she'll hurt you. We're only human, Morgan. Things happen. But with God's guidance and your persistence in your faith, things will work out."

Slowly, Morgan nodded. "I—yeah. Now the question is, what am I going to do?"

"Good question," Ben said and relaxed in the chair and crossed his legs.

"Going near Lindsay is out. That would be underhanded, and as scared as Rachel is right now, it would only aggravate matters."

"I think you're right on that one. Next option."

"I could call her mom—no. That'd look like…" Morgan made a face at Ben.

Ben chuckled. "Copping out? Hey, if I loved the woman, I'd try anything I could to get her back."

"How will Betty feel about this?" Morgan suddenly asked. "She loves her kids, loves Lindsay, too."

"You'll have to ask her that."

Morgan sighed and rubbed the back of his neck where he could feel the muscles twisting. "So first I have to find out if her mother is out to cook my liver for supper. If not, then I have to see if she'll talk to Rachel and maybe gauge how she'd react to me coming by to talk."

"Now that, Morgan, sounds like a plan."

Morgan grinned at Ben. "And, knowing Rachel, when she slams the door in my face, I'll have to find a different way."

"You'll find a way. Stop, listen and wait upon the Lord. It'll come to you. Right now, though—"

The ringing of the phone stopped him. "Excuse me. The job never ends." He smiled at Morgan and stood.

Morgan watched him and thought, how true. Who did you call when you were in need and felt like heaven was not hearing your prayers? Most people would call the preacher. Morgan hadn't ever thought about Ben getting calls like that. Of course, he and Ben had developed a friendship so he automatically bounced his problems off him.

As Morgan watched him, he realized Ben often got calls late at night. This one, though, looked serious.

"I'll check the hospitals and police stations…"

Morgan sat up straighter. Hospitals and police stations?

"I feel it would be best if I did. No, he and I are friends, and I'm sorry you think it's my influence that caused him to run away."

Ben turned. Anger darkened his features. "Of course, Mrs. Erickson. No, Mrs. Erickson. Well, be that as it may, I'm still going to go check. Good night, Mrs. Erickson."

Morgan knew that name. They were one of the families who opposed Ben being in charge of the church. Rich, lived on the outskirts of town. They held the belief that position in town and church were more important than the condition of their souls. Maybe he was wrong on that one. But they spent so much time trying to get slivers out of everyone else's eyes, including those of people who didn't even attend church, that they couldn't see the log in their own—their self-righteousness.

Ben hung up.

"What's up? Can you talk about it?"

Ben nodded and grabbed his jacket off the back of a dining room chair. "Yeah, I can talk. You want to come with me? It seems Jason has run away. And his family is out for my blood for influencing him in rebellious ways."

"Run away? Wait a minute. They're worried about you and what you did?"

"Their way of coping with their fear, I'm sure. Anyway, I want to check the hospitals and police station, the church and a few of his hangouts."

"Of course. I'll go with you, Ben," Morgan said, concern coloring his voice.

Ben paused. "Aw, I'm sorry. We were talking about Rachel. Listen, we can wait on this if you'd like to—"

"No." Morgan shook his head. "No. This is more important. As you said, Rachel isn't going anywhere, for a while at least. And you've helped me more tonight than you have any idea, Ben. I had never gotten over my daughter. Oh, I thought I had, but seeing Rachel's reaction tonight... Believe it or not, it was like a penance for me, finally, to hear what I never heard from my wife—her anger and rage.''

"God doesn't require penance, Morgan.''

"I know. But I think, for me, I had to hear that so I could put the past to rest.''

Ben reached out and clapped him on the shoulder. "God helped you, Morgan. Not me.''

Morgan nodded at Ben. "Let's go.''

His eyes reflecting his gratefulness, Ben nodded.

Morgan only hoped while they were out searching for Jason that Rachel had time to talk to her mom and calm down.

Chapter Twenty

"That was Morgan again."

The quiet creak of the old wooden floor was the only noise as her mother crossed to where Rachel sat at the table working on the last of the financial reports.

"Why won't you talk to him, honey?"

Her mother's voice oozed with concern and worry. It ate Rachel up to hear her mother ask that. "I just can't, Mama. I just can't."

"I think he really loves you," Betty murmured.

"I know," Rachel whispered. Then her gaze went to Lindsay, who was across the room playing with a dollhouse.

"He cares for her, too, honey."

"I—I—" Rachel returned her attention to the ledgers. "I wish I could be sure."

Betty sank into a chair next to her. "Oh, honey, he's not Jim. Why can't you understand that?"

Rachel laid aside her pen and looked up. She knew her eyes reflected the lack of sleep and many tears she'd shed over the past week. She was physically and emotionally exhausted. She needed sleep. "He's exactly like Jim, Mom. He told his wife he didn't want a baby," she whispered the words. "Then he told her his job came first."

"No, honey," her mother said firmly. "He may have been like Jim at one time, but not now. He's changed. And don't forget, his wife deceived him. He was hurt. She was hurt. They didn't deal with it well. And things happened."

"But why? Did he really change? Or is it only temporary, like Jim? As soon as we marry will he turn his back on Lindsay?"

"Honey…" her mother said. Rachel saw the pain in her gaze and heard the distress in her voice.

"I'm taking Lindsay fishing tomorrow. I

need time alone, away from town. I have decisions to make.''

Her mother studied her closely. "You're thinking of leaving, aren't you?''

Rachel's gaze slid to Lindsay.

"You can't run forever, Rachel. Sooner or later you have to face that bad decisions were made and that it's okay to go on. Stop punishing yourself for what Jim did. Stop letting the pain he caused you create a wall between you and God.''

"Mom!''

"Well, it's true. And you know it. God didn't cause these problems. They happened, and you're doing your dead-level best to block what just might be the best step of your life.''

"*Might be* are the words to worry about there, Mother.''

Betty's eyes snapped fire. "If you'd pray and seek God, let go of it, you'd find out just how much He really loves you and that He wants to work this out for the good.''

"What am I supposed to do, Mom? I've asked Him to show me, and what happens? Morgan confesses about his daughter.''

"But he did confess,'' her mother argued.

"But that doesn't tell me that he'd love

Lindsay once we were married. I just need that proof." Rachel bit her lip to keep from sobbing. "Oh, Mama, I just want peace again."

"Oh, honey," Betty whispered. She moved around the table and sat down and took her daughter in her arms.

Rachel sobbed. Her mother prayed. Lindsay bounced over and crawled into her mother's lap and wrapped her arms around her.

Rachel held her close while she tried to get herself under control. It was to no avail. She realized it was God talking to her, trying to get her to let go and turn back to Him. And slowly, as she cried a crack opened up in her heart. No longer was it her mother holding her and comforting her, but it was the soothing words of the Holy Spirit reminding her that He still hadn't left her and was there for her. "Please show me, God," she cried out. "I have to know. I can't go through that again."

With those words she felt a release. Years of pain flowed out, pain she'd harbored against God for allowing her daughter to be born with a hearing problem, pain for her husband running off. Pain for all that had built up within her.

It was nearly an hour later that she stopped

crying. "You're going to bed," Betty said firmly.

"I have work here, Mom," Rachel said. Her head pounded. Her eyes were nearly swollen shut. She couldn't breathe, and her throat was raw. She had never felt so miserable and so exhausted in her life. Nor had she felt so peaceful. Lindsay was asleep in her arms, which now felt like lead from holding her. But her heart was calm where God was concerned. She knew things would be okay. Still, she had to think about Morgan. She had to decide what to do. Tomorrow, alone, fishing, she'd have time to think. Betty took Lindsay, carried her to the sofa and laid her on it for a nap.

"Your work can wait. It's late afternoon. You should rest. You have decisions to make tomorrow and you'll need a clear head. Now, stand up, walk down to your room and go to bed."

Rachel found she was too tired to argue, especially when her mother came over and slipped an arm around her, urging her up. "I can make it."

"I want to tuck my little girl in. Humor me."

Rachel didn't argue. She wanted to be

tucked in. She went into her room, stripped off her pants and top and found a gown. She changed, washed her face and returned to her room. Her mother waited for her.

The covers were turned down. Rachel quietly got into bed.

Betty tenderly tucked the covers around her, leaned down and kissed her on the forehead. "You sleep. I'll watch Lindsay and take care of dinner. That work isn't due until Monday and can wait until Sunday afternoon. I'll wake you up for dinner."

Rachel looked at her mom, her love obvious in her gaze. "Thank you, Mom."

"No more tears," Betty warned when she saw tears starting. "Sleep."

Obediently, Rachel nodded and closed her eyes.

Betty walked across the room and pulled the drapes. Very quietly, Rachel's voice drifted to her. "I love you, Mom."

Betty stood there a moment, her heart breaking over the pain her baby girl was going through. "And I love you, sweetheart," she replied and slipped out of the room.

Pulling the door closed, Betty stood a minute, allowing her hurt and pain to overcome her. When Rachel had married Jim, both Betty and Rachel's dad had been worried something wasn't right about him. Had her father seen how Jim had really treated her, he would have had a heart attack. Instead, a stroke took him before that could happen.

Betty was a go-getter. She didn't believe in sitting around in defeat. But losing her husband had almost devastated her. Had it not been for the people of the church and her job, she wasn't sure she could have made it. The best years of her life had been with her husband.

True, she had found a life after her husband. But now she'd met Warren and had a chance at a new and different job. Warren was... Warren. He wasn't like her husband. He was just Warren. And she loved him.

And she wanted Rachel to have that love, too. Just as she'd wanted Pastor Ben and Julianne to get together, but rumor had it they'd decided to only be friends. Kids nowadays. They just couldn't do it by themselves. If she left it to her stubborn daughter and that moping doctor who refused just to come over here and drag Rachel to the altar, then neither one of them would fix their problems. Now that Rachel's heart was right with God, things could proceed.

Betty grinned. She had the perfect way to get them together. And it wasn't going to be after Rachel decided to leave Fairweather. She quietly went downstairs to the kitchen and dialed the phone.

Chapter Twenty-One

"Twenty-two to fourteen."

Morgan leaned down and dropped his hands to his knees. He was soaked with sweat and breathing heavily. "You were right, basketball is a good way to think out problems."

Ben chuckled. "And you thought I only played it as goodwill for kids." Tossing the ball, he made another basket.

"Hey, that one doesn't count."

Ben chuckled, caught the ball and jogged to Morgan. "So, what have you decided about Rachel?"

Morgan stared at him, then scowled, took the ball and bounced it before tossing it at the hoop—and missing.

"You know, when you avoid that question you always miss," Ben observed.

"You're too observant," Morgan muttered, and lobbed the ball at him.

Ben caught it with a grunt. "You said you rarely play basketball," he murmured.

"It's the question that gives me the aim," Morgan retorted.

Ben laughed and bounced it, tossed it and made another basket.

Morgan caught the rebound and moved. Looking at Ben, he finally sighed. "I've tried all week to get in contact with her. She won't take calls. She doesn't leave her house, according to Betty. What am I going to do, barge in and demand to see her?"

"Well, now, that's not exactly right," Ben said, and motioned at him. "Throw it."

"Such technical terms," Morgan said dryly, and bounced it.

Just as he aimed and started to toss the ball, Ben said, "Rachel isn't home right now."

The ball soared off target, hitting the edge of the backboard and flying.

Ben shot over and caught it.

Morgan groaned. "Funny, Reverend. Really funny."

Instead of shooting, Ben slipped the ball under his arm and walked forward. "I'm not kidding. Betty told me last night that Rachel was going fishing with Lindsay today. And Betty also told me she hasn't given the medical report about Lindsay to Rachel yet. She said, if I remember her words correctly, 'You are the doctor and Lindsay is her granddaughter and you should be giving the report to the mother, not the grandmother.'"

Morgan stared, stunned. "She hasn't told her the findings yet?"

Slowly Ben shook his head. "I think, from what she hinted, she wanted you to go out to the fishing pond and deliver the news yourself."

"Which pond?" Morgan demanded.

Ben shrugged. "Betty didn't say. She did say that Rachel was sentimental, though."

Morgan hesitated, then smiled. "Thanks, Ben." He punched the ball, knocking it out of Ben's hands. With a quick dribble, he lobbed it and made a basket. "I'll have to play this game with you more often," he murmured. "Gotta go now, though."

He grabbed his T-shirt, slipped it on and headed toward his car.

Ben grinned, thinking Betty had been right. All Morgan needed was the chance to see Rachel alone, and those medical records would provide the excuse. With an innocent whistle, Ben tossed the ball. "Basket," he murmured, and a slow smile turned up the corners of his mouth.

Morgan didn't take time to go home and shower and change. He drove straight to the pond he'd taken Rachel and Lindsay to weeks ago. Sentimental. Morgan was certain that meant Rachel was thinking of him, of what had happened and maybe, just maybe, if she was here, then that meant she was thinking of the good times they'd shared. And with the good news and bad news he had, at least that would give him a reason to be there.

He turned onto the rutted road, and bumped along until he came to a clearing.

She had heard him coming.

She was facing the road, staring. And there was Lindsay, playing in an ice chest. She must have caught another fish. Morgan smiled softly. His heart expanded. He loved them. He wasn't going to leave here until he convinced Rachel of that. "Okay, Father. Here we go. It's in Your court. Help me convince Rachel that I love her and I'm not going to leave Lindsay, no matter what.''

He pulled to a stop, put the parking break on and shoved open the door, leaving the keys in the car. Then he stood and rested his arms on the door. ''Hello, Rachel.''

''Hello, Morgan.''

She stood four feet away from her daughter, staring at him.

She was a sight for sore eyes. ''You look like death warmed over,'' he murmured.

''You don't look any better,'' she said defensively.

''Fissee!'' Lindsay said, and came running.

Rachel started to prevent her daughter then shot him a frantic look.

''I'm not going to hurt her, Rachel.''

He followed Lindsay over to look at the fish and ooh and ah over it before turning back to Rachel.

She had moved to the tree and was packing up the lunch basket. Morgan went over to her. ''We have to talk.''

''I don't want to talk,'' she whispered, her gaze down, refusing to look at him.

''I know, honey. And if it wasn't so important, I'd let it go. But I love you, and I love that little girl over there. I've been patient for a week. After all, I dropped one of the worst bombshells possible on you at the worst possible time. So I owed you that much. But I just can't let you go.''

Rachel looked up. The torment in her eyes tore at his heart. "I don't have any choice. I have to let you go."

"Why, Rachel?" he asked calmly. Strangely, he was at peace as he spoke with her. He wanted her to be honest, tell him what was the matter so maybe he could help her. Help Lindsay.

"I…"

When she hesitated, he pressured her gently. "You love me. You said you did." He took her hand. "Don't you, Rachel?"

"You know I do," she whispered, and her voice broke. "I didn't think I'd ever love anyone again. But I do. I fell without even realizing it until it was too late. But…"

"But what?" He encouraged her, knowing exactly what but wanting her to say it.

"But I just can't, not after the way Jim used me, tricked me. My judgment isn't the best in the world. I can't risk marrying you and you coming to regret Lindsay or wanting to send her off.''

"I don't want that, Rachel. Not at all.''

He meant it. He saw the struggle in her eyes, her need to believe. But she couldn't accept it. "Why do you love her? Is she a replacement for your daughter? Is that it?''

Morgan nodded. "Maybe at first she was. Maybe that's why I decided to be a pediatrician after my daughter's death. Maybe I have been trying to pay for what I did through each patient. But not Lindsay. At least not now. She reached inside and wrapped herself around my heart.''

"I—oh, Morgan, I wish I could believe that. I just—at the first sign of trouble…''

When she didn't go on, he changed the subject. "I have the reports back on Lindsay.''

"You do?''

He saw the banked hope. He hated to disappoint her. "Her hearing disability isn't reversible, honey. I'm sorry.''

Her shoulders sagged.

"However," he added, "the tests show her hearing range and just what she's hearing. And Rachel, I think, with some special hearing aids, that Lindsay's hearing could probably improve fifty percent. Which would mean she would be able to hear and understand and probably with speech therapy talk normally.''

Rachel stared. ''The other doctor never suggested hearing aids.''

''He was a fool.''

Rachel hesitated and nibbled her lip. ''I...that's wonderful. But, Morgan—''

''It's okay, love. Don't think I'm telling you this to sway how you feel about me. I've prayed and I believe God opens doors and eventually you're going to realize I love you and won't leave—''

''Lindsay!'' Rachel's eyes widened in horror, and she screamed, a high, shrill scream that sent the hairs on the back of his neck standing straight up.

Whirling, he saw what had her paralyzed with terror. Lindsay stood near the water, blood dripping down her head, her face white, eyes round. They both jumped into action.

Rachel ran to Lindsay, reaching her at the same time he did. Grabbing her daughter, she cried, ''Lindsay, Lindsay, oh, baby...''

''Rachel!'' Morgan commanded, having no idea how he spoke. He was trembling at seeing the little child covered in blood.

"She's bleeding," Rachel cried. She pushed Lindsay's hair back, and a two-inch cut was revealed. "She fell. I—I don't know—there's so much blood!"

"Rachel!" he commanded again. "Give her to me."

The authority in his voice reached her, and she released Lindsay.

"Hey there, sweetheart," he murmured.

Lindsay burst into loud wails and threw her arms around him. Like a leech, Lindsay attached her arms and legs to him. "She's going to need sutures. I have a bag in the car. But it'd be better if we took her to the hospital for this," he said, and stood. "Think you can drive?"

Nodding, she stood, then rushed toward his car. Of all the times to forget his cell phone and pager. They were still at Ben's in his house. Morgan stood with Lindsay in his arms and hurried to his car.

"She's all bloody," Rachel whimpered.

"She'll be fine," Morgan murmured.

"I should have been paying attention to her. She's a handful sometimes but, oh, Morgan, I love her so much."

Rachel started the car and took off. When

she hit the highway, though she sped, she drove calmly and safely. "I do, too," he said softly, even as Lindsay started to calm. "She's going to have a headache. But she'll be okay. She evidently tripped and hit her head, Rachel. It was no one's fault. Sometimes things like this happen. You can't foresee things like this, just like I couldn't foresee what my wife would do, Rachel."

Rachel's gaze jerked quickly to Morgan before she looked back to the road. "Like I couldn't foresee how Jim was going to change."

Rachel parked at the ER. Morgan slipped out of the car with Lindsay in his arms. Rachel was right behind him. He took Lindsay to a trauma room, snapping out a description of Lindsay's injury to the doctor on duty.

Then Morgan backed out of the room.

"Wait!" Rachel said. "What are you doing? Don't leave her in there!"

Morgan wrapped his arms around her. "Come on. You can't stay here. We have to go to the waiting room."

Rachel shook her head. "You're her doctor. You have to be in there with her. I—I trust you with her."

He caught her hands, brought them to his mouth and kissed them. "Honey, I can't go in there." He imagined his words seemed odd, considering he was smiling so softly. He couldn't help it. Her words wrapped around his heart like a healing salve in an open wound.

"But why?" she demanded, confused.

His emotion obvious in his voice, he said, "Because I love her as if she were my own, and the first thing you're taught in medical school is never to work on someone you love."

Chapter Twenty-Two

Morgan wasn't sure Rachel heard him. Suddenly she dissolved in his arms and held him close.

He wrapped his arms around her and guided her to the waiting room. Then he sat down, pulled Rachel onto his lap and cuddled her close.

"Did you mean it when you said you loved me, Rachel?" Morgan asked.

Her tiny body, nestled so close to him, felt so right, so perfect. He didn't think he could take her rejection if she said no.

"Yes." The answer was a mere breath of air whispered past his ear. But it sounded as loud as the Liberty Bell. It flowed through his entire being, bringing a rush of relief and joy.

Ben came striding toward them before Morgan could answer. Fairweather was a small town. Everyone knew everyone. The nurses here knew Morgan went to Ben's church. They knew Betty, probably Rachel, too. It was inevitable that someone would call Ben.

"How is Lindsay?" he asked, stopping before them and kneeling, sliding a hand to Rachel's back.

"She only conked her head, Ben. She's probably getting sutures at the moment."

"Well, that's a relief. Someone called saying you'd brought her in and she was covered in blood and dying."

"Gossips," Morgan said affectionately. "Concerned, at least." He gave Ben a significant look, and Ben, eyes widening, nodded and backed off.

He returned his attention to Rachel. "And I wasn't lying when I said I loved you, darling."

She tilted her head, and her red-rimmed eyes met his gaze. She must have accepted the love she saw in them because fresh tears welled and slipped over. "Oh, Morgan."

"And I love Lindsay. How could I not?"

The ER doctor came out into the waiting room, rubbing the back of his neck. "Lindsay there is one lucky little girl. She's going to be okay. As soon as we get her cleaned up, you can go in. Twelve stitches that child held. Nasty."

Rachel cried in utter relief. Morgan smiled at the doctor. "Thanks Jerry."

Jerry smiled, his eyes twinkling. "This is the type of news I like to give. If you'll excuse me, I have to go write some orders."

Ben moved to the pay phone, giving them some privacy.

Rachel hugged him close. "Oh, Morgan, I've been such a fool."

Morgan returned the embrace. "Oh? How's that, sweetheart?"

"I love you more than life itself. You're nothing like Jim. Maybe at one time you made a mistake, but God forgives, and I have no right to hold something against you that you were brave enough to tell me."

Morgan's heart expanded with love. "Yes, love. I will never hide anything from you. That would only defeat marriage. I'll always be honest with you. And that's all I'd ask in return, for you to be honest with me."

"How can you still care after what I've put you through this last week?"

Morgan smoothed her hair and rocked her in his arms. "You were scared, out of control."

She nodded against his chest. "I just didn't realize God's in control, Morgan, even when we can't see it."

"Yes, He is, sweetheart."

She cupped his cheek, her soft hand warm and gentle against his stubble.

"Does this mean you'll marry me?" he asked, grinning at her, though he was serious as his gaze searched her face.

"Does this mean you're asking?" Her eyes shone with love and joy. There was acceptance there and, yes, love. Love for him.

Morgan grinned, allowing the joy to bubble over inside him. She was his! He was hers! Thank you, God! "I haven't asked you, have I?" he teased.

"Well…" she began. He stood and sat her in the chair. Rachel blinked. "Morgan? What—"

Dropping down on one knee, he took her hand in both of his.

All conversation around them suddenly

stopped. Ben, who was talking on the phone to Betty, started whispering as he watched. Even the people at the nurse's station quieted to see why the noisy waiting room had gone silent.

Morgan grinned. "Fairest lady in all of this earthly kingdom, I announce my love to you and these witnesses here. I would gladly slay any dragons for you, climb any mountains and mow any yard."

Rachel giggled. "Morgan!" Her cheeks heated up to pink, and his naughty grin widened.

"To you, Rachel, I give you my heart, when I tell you I love you and wish you to be my wife for now and forever more. What say you, Rachel Anderson White? Will you do me the honor of becoming Rachel Anderson White Talbot? Or will you slay my heart, leaving it bleeding and in pieces?"

Slowly, she shook her head. "Never, my love. But I won't be Rachel Anderson White Talbot."

His heart plummeted. The people around them gasped. Then she smiled. "But I will become just Rachel Talbot."

A cheer went up.

Morgan stood and pulled her into his arms. "Very well, then, Just Rachel Talbot."

And there, in front of the citizens of Fairweather, Minnesota, they sealed their vows with a kiss.

*   *   *   *   *

If you enjoyed reading

WHAT THE DOCTOR ORDERED,

you'll love…

TWIN WISHES

by Kathryn Alexander, the second book in the FAIRWEATHER series.

On sale March 2000

Dear Reader,

When Love Inspired asked me to write this book, I was stunned and excited. When I found out what it was about, I just knew that God had a hand in it. You see, I was fifteen when my best friend, Teresa, had a child born with cytomegalovirus and total deafness. I grew up loving Steven Haynes as much as I loved his mom. In college, I studied to be a nurse. I was an EMT Advanced (IP in some states). I met my husband there and married. We decided to have children, and as much as I loved the medical field, I wanted to be with my children more. It was a true sacrifice, a love I never lost. When we moved to Louisiana, I got involved in bus ministry and met two wonderful children, Joey and Heather Thomas. Both were deaf. Through them, I experienced a whole new world as I learned slang sign language that I didn't even know existed (ask me sometime how to say airhead)!

That's why Lindsay is so special to me. Teresa is why the mother, Rachel, holds my heart. And Morgan, well, let's just say he's a bit of all the best doctors rolled into one. Thank you, Love Inspired, for the honor of writing this book and thank you, dear readers, for contacting me to let me know what you think of it.

Cheryl Wolverton